CHOOSE ME

ALSO BY EVELYN LAU

CHOOSE ME

Stories

EVELYN LAU

VINTAGE CANADA

A Division of Random House of Canada Limited

Vintage Canada and colophon are registered trademarks of Random House of Canada Limited.

Canadian Cataloguing in Publication Data

Lau, Evelyn, 1971–
  Choose me

ISBN 0-385-25849-6

I. Title.

PS8573.A7815C46 1999   C813'.54   C98-932853-8
PR9199.3.L38C46 1999

Published in Canada by Vintage Canada, a division of
Random House of Canada Limited

Printed and bound in Canada

TRAN 10 9 8 7 6 5 4 3 2 1

This is a work of fiction; the characters and settings found within are imaginary composites and do not refer to actual persons or places.

in memory

CONTENTS

But for some reason love, even of the most ardent and soul-destroying kind, is never caught by the lens of the camera. One would almost think it didn't exist.

— William Maxwell, *So Long, See You Tomorrow*

FAMILY

ZOE STOOD IN Douglas's bedroom, the one he shared with his wife. Outside the wood-framed window the afternoon was silver, the sky the shine of the inside of an oyster shell. Snow drifted through the air, and narrow icicles hung from the trees. The houses dwindling down the block were heritage properties, fronted in brick and stained glass; each resembled the house she was inside.

Douglas had invited her in so calmly. After she set down her bags in the hall with its high ceilings and polished floors, he pushed the keys to his home into her hand, two skeleton keys dangling from a loop of twisted wire. Then he motioned her back out onto the porch, where he wrapped his fingers around hers, demonstrating how to work the locks. Their breath showed in front of them, but his hand pulsed with warmth. She learned to shove the keys in smoothly, to jiggle them, to listen for the muffled internal click that signified the lock had been turned.

"Will you remember this?"

He repeated the code to the burglar alarm by the door, half-concealed by the winter coats hanging on the wooden rack.

"Yes. I think I'll remember."

His wife appeared on the landing at the top of the stairs.

"Ellen, this is our visiting poet, Zoe. She's been on campus all week working with the students, and I thought it'd be nice for her to stay in a real home before she leaves, especially since we won't be here."

Ellen came down the first flight of stairs, bending to extend her hand; her arm was long, her palm warm.

"Welcome."

Zoe held his wife's hand in her own and swallowed past the catch in her throat. His wife continued to lean down from the landing, bending her body from the waist, one hand holding the railing, the other clasping Zoe's as though to help her up. Douglas kept his eyes fastened on Ellen's face. Their two children were clamouring around her, tugging and demanding; the girl jumped up and down, whining, while the boy pulled down his trousers to reveal buttocks as smooth as cream.

"Jason, I said no. Look, we have a guest. Say hello, Jason, say hello to Zoe."

The boy ignored her, burying his face in his mother's thigh, squirming his bare bum in the air while his sister hid behind them both.

"Zoe will be staying here while we're at the cabin. You've got to be good and say hello."

After a while, just when it seemed he could not be persuaded, Jason lifted his face and grinned winningly. His eyes were like his father's, only clearer, the colour of amber.

"Hello. Hello!" he shouted.

Douglas pressed the keys once more into her palm. She looked at him then in a moment of terror, the weight and light of the house around her suddenly there for her to both protect and invade. He sensed her fear, mistook it for concern about burglar alarms, difficult locks, the house burning down.

"Got it?"

He repeated the code again.

"Is everything all right? Are you happy?"

He had given her the keys, his hands were empty. At the top of the stairs his wife was saying, "No, no, no," to the children. "No, you *can't* bring that. Look, you already have so much."

"I'm happy."

She stood in the doorway and watched him leave with his family. Ellen was weighted with the children's clothes, warm and puffy jackets that were awkward in her arms. Jason and Julia ran ahead, the tops of their heads bright and new in the winter light. Douglas paused before following them; he placed both his hands on Zoe's upper arms and kissed her on the cheek.

"One more."

He kissed her on the other cheek just as she was pulling away.

She looked over his shoulder and caught the blur of Ellen's face. She felt the sudden tension, her body electric with watchfulness. But the moment passed quickly—it was only a kiss, friendly, sociable. Ellen beamed and waved.

"Have a good time!"

"You too!"

She eased the door shut, the house was hers.

Zoe approached their bed as though it were an altar. It was smooth, flat, wide—a square of white in the room. She sat on its edge, where the comforter was folded back in a triangle, and the cotton sheet slid against her body. She could tell by the paraphernalia on the bedside table, the textbooks and manuscripts piled high, which side of the bed was his.

She wondered what Ellen looked like naked, how she approached him in the dark with the light from the window illuminating her body. Ellen had the figure of an adolescent, long and boyishly thin; her breasts would hardly be more than bumps on her chest, bare mouthfuls, and the bones in her hips and pubis would be prominent, traceable. The length of her would look like a white taper candle, if he opened his eyes in the night to watch her sleep.

Their bedroom was full of photographs—lined up on the mantel, jumbled above the chest of drawers, taped to the vanity mirror. The pictures were almost all of Douglas and the children; in the few where Ellen was present, her face was either obscured by her blowing hair or turned to one side, away from the camera. She appeared in the photos as a sort of ghost, rinsed of ego, her features blurred. It was Douglas who took centre stage, which was why Zoe had the impression when she saw them together on the stairs that he was the more attractive of the two. And yet when she looked again, objectively, she realized she was wrong—it was Ellen who was most attractive. Her face was white and well shaped, like a Madonna's, graceful and open. Her teeth glistened when she smiled. But Douglas had something she lacked, a force of personality that was revealed in the photographs, the same photos that revealed Ellen's downturned, devolving features.

Their family life was documented in the photographs. Douglas, Ellen and the children had taken summer holidays by the shore, stood in portals of museums and crumbling European buildings, hiked among shrub and rock and cliff. In one photograph he held his daughter spilling and giggling over his shoulder while he pointed, laughing, at the camera. In another his face was white with joy as he cradled a swaddled newborn in his arms. In a third he was naked to the waist at the beach, his feet buried in wet sand that flowered around his ankles; she saw the arc of his shoulders, the way he was shaped and curved, and the twin lines of his waist that sloped inwards. He was someplace where her own history was not, could never be.

When Zoe opened his wife's closet doors she saw loose,

layered clothes in deep jewel colours. The surface of the vanity next to the closet was scattered with drugstore cosmetics and, incongruously, a shiny, unopened bottle of Chanel No. 5 which must have been a gift. Her eye pencils were worn down to blurred nubs, her tube of mascara was dusty, she owned only the palest of lipsticks. This was the sort of woman his wife was, Zoe realized—natural, unselfconscious, without guile.

The house was old enough to be draughty, the heaters thin and metallic and cool to the touch. The walls were papered in a pattern of wide bronze stripes; the floorboards were stained walnut. That night she woke in their bedroom, curled to Douglas's side of the bed, shivering. She tiptoed across the icy floor to the dresser where one of Ellen's nightshirts hung from a knob; its worn cotton, smelling faintly of soap, was soft against her skin when she pulled it over her head. She wondered how Douglas was sleeping in his cabin. Were his arms wrapped around his wife, her stomach, her breasts? He was the warmest man she had ever met—his mouth, his hands, the heat barely contained by the skin of his body. To kiss him was like leaning her face over a hot stove, or into a fire. By comparison, she was cold, or he said, cold-blooded.

"Now I know why you came wearing so few clothes, it's because you're cold-blooded."

But she wore few clothes so that when he touched her, it would be that much more. So that when he took her hand from her lap and lifted it to his mouth, or held it between his own hands, the shock of his heat would be greater. It was deliberate. She had been freezing the whole week, at all the places he had taken her when she was not lecturing to students. When they had stood in the organic-foods market with their hands in their pockets, the breath issuing whitely in front of them, watching the butcher in his bloody apron behind the counter. The chopping blade that fit so firmly into his hand it was like an extension of him. Turkeys, pheasants, a dead deer hung by their hind legs in front of the shop, freshly killed. She imagined their bodies still warm, hearts still beating, had to resist the urge to lean forward and stroke her fingertips down the grain of their feathers and fur, towards the belly warm as the belly of a sleeping man. They were so beautiful, content. The turkeys' creamy eyelids tugged down over their eyes, their closed beaks bearing tremblingly a single drop of blood. They had stood together, side by side, looking at the dead animals strung silently in front of them. To see then his breath steaming beside hers, to know his hands were warm and alive in his pockets, composed of skin and flesh and bone and circulating blood, to see the flicker of his eyelashes, to know he was swallowing and breathing and thinking and wondering, to know that if she leaned into his chest she would hear the pulse of his heart—it was almost more than she could bear.

To drive back to the campus at night with the whole of the highway before them, the planes skimming low with their lit wings towards the airport, the singing stream of traffic, the gas stations along the way with their pumps and phone booths and chocolate bars, the dense black tar of the road painted with lines and signals. His hands on the wheel and then his thumb on the fleshy pocket between her own thumb and forefinger, touching just that part of her, and the balletic perfection of the traffic around them, orange and red taillights sliding past, speeding forward, the coordination of motion, the sense of at last being a part of something whole, his hand wrapping around her hand.

One day they had stood in a church tower with many windows and walked around and around to take in each disparate view. From here the emerald sea shaking in the distance like a mirage, from there the city with its multiple windows gleaming in the golden light. It had taken them fifteen minutes to climb to the top of the tower, the stairs so steep they had had to twist their bodies nearly sideways, so sharply angled that the steps above bit into their shins. And then they had emerged onto the wooden platform with the light flooding in from all directions, and they had stepped from window to window as though they were dancing, and when they stood next to each other the fringe of his scarf touched the shoulder of her sweater.

Then they had paused in the entrance of the church, overwhelmed by a window of stained glass. They had whispered to each other and he had wanted to touch her, she saw that, the times when he wanted to touch her, the look that came over his face, how it was turned to her beneath the flood of coloured light and how she had seen the thought in his eyes, his eyes that moved back and forth when he was thinking as though he were scanning the lines of a secret text.

The weekend passed slowly. After Zoe had wandered all the rooms in the house, picking up objects here and there, inspecting and then setting them down again, there was nothing more for her to do. So she was grateful when Douglas's associate at the publishing company called to invite her for lunch. He took her to a Wolfgang Puck restaurant with slender cedar chairs, papaya-coloured walls and preternaturally beautiful women whose heels clicked across the granite floor. During lunch she observed this man's gentleness—his patience with the waiters, his smiling consideration of her—and it made her sad. He was someone she could trust, the way she never would be able to trust Douglas. As they ate their scallop salads, she thought of the afternoon in the French restaurant with the brown and yellow tiles on the floor, when Douglas had made her translate the entire menu. She knew only a little French and he had had to correct her and help her along, from the starters to the specials to the entrées to the desserts, all the way down the menu, not letting her stop.

"How will you know what you want if you don't know what there is?"

What he said was true, so she kept translating. The waiters

came and he waved them away. The other diners must have thought they were lovers, because of the way they looked at each other. The tables were set close together, there was no privacy; the women around them had wide mouths and espresso-coloured hair, and the nails that tipped their long fingers were manicured. Cellular phones rang at the tables of the men, who wore suit jackets over jeans. They'd ordered a bottle of wine with their meal, and the first glass of it rushed to her head. She could not pick out her own face in the strip of mirror that ran along the wall above the booths, not among so many faces crowded together. Since childhood it had been necessary for Zoe to see her reflection at all times, as if to assure herself of her own existence. When she tried to find herself in the mirror in the restaurant and could not, she drank the wine instead, to calm herself.

"Zoe, everything I've ever done in my life has been like an experiment. It started when I was a child. The way I looked at the world was different from the children around me. I was very observant, and because of that I felt removed from everything. I began to direct my own life. As a teenager, I experimented with drugs because I wanted to understand what it was like to lose control. And then I made myself fall in love over and over, for the same reason."

She watched him; everything he said made sense to her. He might have been describing her own past. But it was what was familiar in him that was dangerous to her.

He had chosen this restaurant from all the restaurants that lined the busy, taxi-filled street. They had stood on the corner and he had looked in either direction and then he had chosen this place.

"I know where we'll go. Come, follow me."

They crossed the murderous intersection, shiny cars veering in front and behind them. The stores all along the street were glass-fronted, etched with the names of Italian designers and filled with expensive merchandise—leaden suits, transparent dresses, shoes built with as much attention as one would give to the building of houses.

He let the waiter show them to the table where he had begun and ended relationships with other women. Now she was sitting on the plump red banquette where his other women had fitted their hips.

He was still talking. The women at the next table turned and looked at them. Zoe smiled. The women blinked their heavy lashes and after a while turned back to their salads.

"You seem closed to me. I don't know how to get close to you, other than to become so important to you that you fall in love with me."

Zoe let him talk.

"You aren't like anyone who is close to me. The people I value don't have centres that are so solid. I can enter them, they're vulnerable to me."

But she still could not pick out her face in the mirror.

Could it be that he was mistaken, that she had no centre, only a space?

After lunch he took her to the downtown publishing office where he worked part-time as an editor. Walking against the direction of the wind, they passed a vendor with his wheelbarrow of roses and carnations, and a café with wrought-iron chairs arranged in circles around outdoor tables. The door to his building was covered in stained glass. He pushed it open, and they walked across a cracked marble floor to the elevator. In the elevator she was struck by a desire to kiss him, but he was already thinking about the work that had accumulated while they were eating. She was drunk only in the way that wine can make you drunk at noon. The angles of the building seemed wrong. The surfaces of things—the metal of desks and elevator doors, the cloth-covered partitions, the lenses of a secretary's glasses as she walked past—all seemed exceptionally bright and sharp. She thought her intoxication must be evident to others, yet there was not a flicker of suspicion or concern in any of the faces that tilted at her, with their black pupils and razor-sharp haircuts. Meanwhile he had vanished into the maze of offices, and left her on her own. She wandered towards the reception area and sat on the couch that curved like a crescent moon. The receptionists were carrying on conversations about clothes and lovers, in between the ringing phones.

When he was with her at dinner, even when there were others at their table, academics and editors, he watched her constantly. She saw him always at the edge of her vision, a pale, intense man in a tailored coat. While she talked to others around her, drank a glass of wine, placed her order with the waiter, she felt his eyes upon her. When at last she raised her eyes to his, he would not flinch away, he would only slowly turn his head to the side—as if she had been merely an object in the way of his turning gaze, as if all along he had been meaning to look at the edge of the table, or the spoon that lay on his saucer, or at another woman. This was how the nights of the previous week had passed, in restaurants where the windows were frosted over so that the night outside looked like it was walled in fog, with only the faint light of streetlamps to mark the distances. At their table, there were always people who drank too much, and she was one of them. At the end of the evening they would be drinking flaming shooters and daring each other to keep up, and she would, because when she tried to back down, looking to Douglas for help, he would stir sugar into his coffee and look back at her and not say anything. When she swallowed the contents of a shot glass in one throw of the wrist, the sensation was like dropping through a hole that had suddenly opened up in the sidewalk. Tears would rise in her eyes and she would feel separated from herself. But when her vision cleared he would still be there at the table, his face empty of reproach or encouragement, only mildly curious as to what she would do next. Later, he would tell her what she was like with other people.

"You manipulate them, you draw them along with you. There is something about you that people can't resist."

He would watch her until the early hours of the morning, when empty shooter glasses lined the tabletop and the party disbanded to stumble through the streets with the fog winding above, the thick heels of their shoes sounding on the cement.

In turn she wanted to believe he was the most genuine person she had ever met. In the market in front of the dead animals when his breath steamed out of him and he spread his arms in wonder. In the car when he sang along with the radio and thumped the wheel and then turned and looked at her as they sat stalled in the black, runny streets. The noises he made when he was thinking, his fingers on the Powerbook keyboard, his head cocked to one side.

"*Tinka tinka tinka. Vroom.*"

He was a grown man, but when he was working he sounded like a child shoving toy race cars down a rubber track. So that one afternoon when they were walking down the street, when for an instant the sun broke through the layers of cloud, she had been astonished to see that his hair was peppered with silver. It was as though someone had taken a handful of needles and scattered them through his dark hair.

He would talk to the words that appeared on his computer screen, give the desk a small slap, wheel around in his chair.

"Yes. Done. Now, where would you like to go for lunch? What would you most like to eat in the whole wide world?"

They would smile at each other and she would see him slowly grow back into himself, see the work fade from his eyes, one wave receding and a different one advancing. He would rise from his chair and stand for a moment with his feet pressed together and his hands clasped behind his back, like someone at the edge of a diving board gazing into the pool, puzzling the point of entry, the locus where his body would knife into the water. She would watch him slowly come back to life the way she had begun to feel her own body assume its life, starting at the nucleus where his hands lay hot on her skin.

During the hours when she was alone in the house, Zoe wondered why Douglas had brought her here, when so much could go wrong. Was it enough that she was in his house, even if he could not be there with her? It was possible he had invited her only out of kindness and affection; after all, he had kissed her boldly on both sides of her face while his wife had watched them from the cobblestone path. Perhaps he felt they had nothing to hide. But she felt that to believe that would be to believe the world itself lacked intelligence and motive. Perhaps he only wanted to see what would happen, to observe his own emotions, his capacity for betrayal or loyalty. And to learn about her capacity for transgression. She saw then that he was the sort of man a woman should never love. Yet she walked about his house in a sort of drunkenness, his home where he lived and ate and slept, and she could almost feel the air parting and streaming around her, the pattern of its current, like she was moving in the corridors of space he had created for her with his own movements. She stood by the sink where he shaved and brushed each morning. She saw his black suit hanging in the bedroom closet, his sneakers flung to the bottom of the wardrobe, the book he was reading lying open on the braided mat that covered the bedside table. Sitting on the edge of their white bed, she felt looming inside her the inevitability of betrayal. It rose in her like the tide, leaving her without will. She knew that as soon as she slept with Douglas in his own house, she would feel relief. She craved it like a junkie; she could taste in her mouth the effects of the drug before it was injected. It would be sweet, his caresses on her body, the pain they would inflict upon his wife.

Once during the weekend the telephone rang for Ellen. Zoe answered it in their bedroom.

"Hello?"

"Ellen? It's Diane. How are you?"

"No. No, Ellen is away for the weekend with the family. Could I take a message?"

When she put down the phone, Zoe rose from their bed and looked at her reflection in their vanity mirror. She put her hand on her neck, felt the shape of her throat with her fingers. Her voice when it came out in the cold room was still hers, accompanied by a thin jet of white breath. She was still herself. She was not his wife.

The day the family came home Zoe woke to the sound of church bells filling the air. The sky was blue and the house so icy she wandered the rooms in a daze, her fingers clenched, her lips chapped. In the bathroom mirror her skin appeared exceptionally pale, stretched over a framework of bone, and the backs of her hands were translucent. She went downstairs to the living room and opened the curtains to look out onto the street. The occupants of the neighbouring houses could be seen here and there in their weekend sweats and denims, climbing into cars, conversing on doorsteps, carrying plastic bins of garbage to the curb. She felt far away from the domestic lives locked within houses such as these and had to remind herself that today, at least, she was on the inside looking out. The hours passed, afternoon darkened into winter evening, and still she waited for Douglas and Ellen. When their car pulled up to the front of the house and they came out with the children, hurrying up the path, she went to the door and let them in as though they were her guests.

"Tell me all about it. What did you do while we were gone?"

His wife was upstairs, putting the children to bed. Zoe heard their footsteps back and forth between the rooms—Ellen's long, purposeful strides, the children's patter. Douglas rose from the sofa to shut the living-room door, and before returning to his seat he detoured to Zoe's chair and ruffled her hair with one hand. He laughed, a self-conscious sound that he bit off quickly. She was so nervous that her upper lip was slick with perspiration, but she said it anyway.

"I missed you horribly."

For the moment he said nothing, but he could not look at her, and that in itself seemed a declaration. They were both saved by the sound of his wife's footsteps down the long stairs, the turn of the doorknob, her presence in the room. Ellen chose the other armchair, the one identical to Zoe's, which also faced the sofa where Douglas sat. Zoe knew that at some point he would not be able to refrain from comparing them, and saw to her surprise that his wife knew this also, by the sudden sharpening of her eyes. Still, it was easy to start a conversation with Ellen. Zoe, to hide her panic, was vivacious and charming, and they talked comfortably about books, children, movies, travel. Douglas became superfluous; he sat back in the sofa and watched them, perhaps for the first time aware of who he had brought into his home, of what she was capable. He saw his own wife warm towards the other woman, saw her caution evaporate, her limbs relax and loosen. When he left the room to escape to his office upstairs, it seemed that neither woman would notice or miss him. But Zoe watched his exit with the care of someone who is making a plan.

"I've got a pile of unmarked essays sitting upstairs. I'll be back down in a while to say goodnight."

Ellen glanced up at her husband.

"I'm not planning to stay up late, Douglas. An hour at most, then I'm coming upstairs and falling into bed. You two can chat down here if you want."

Douglas and Zoe did not look at each other.

"Well, anyway. Don't worry about making noise, I'll be fast asleep."

Douglas left the room, closing the door behind him. Ellen turned towards Zoe, cradling her drink near her knee, her face lit by the lamp on the sidetable. They continued to talk for a while, and the conversation turned towards her marriage.

"I was looking at some of the photos in the house," Zoe said. "The two of you, and the children—you have such a wonderful family. I couldn't believe how different Douglas looked when he was younger."

"Yes, I was so in love with him when we first got together. He was beautiful."

Her eyes wrinkled with the memory, and a distant pleasure swept over Ellen's face, softening it, making it vulnerable.

"I thought so, too."

"Did you? Well, he's older now. But you saw how he used to have the most beautiful long curls. He was a gorgeous young man, I can't tell you. Sometimes I have to remind myself of the way he used to be."

"But could you imagine yourself with anyone else? I mean, is he your great love, your grand passion?"

The moment of consideration was so slight as to not be there. Then his wife was nodding, smiling.

"Yes. Yes, he is. You know, once when we were still going out, he left me for a year. I couldn't eat, I couldn't sleep, I thought I was going to die. I heard through mutual friends that he was living with another woman, and I couldn't bear it. I wanted to have his children. I couldn't imagine my life without him."

They were silent for a while. On the back of her neck Zoe felt the heat of the lamp behind her chair, and a line of perspiration travelled down her temple. The rest of the room was still cold but she was burning up. The bottle of whisky on the occasional table between them was half empty, and she realized that she had been doing most of the drinking. Ellen gazed into her own glass, the thin, slippery line of alcohol left at its bottom.

"Anyway. I really must get to bed, it all starts again tomorrow. I have to be up early to make the children's breakfast and get them ready. I'll wake you if you want."

"Please. I don't want to miss my flight."

Ellen unfolded her legs and stood up. The skin around her eyes had crumpled with exhaustion. She smiled at her guest.

"Thank you. I've enjoyed our talk, Zoe. I feel as if I've made a new friend."

"Goodnight."

Zoe was left alone for a few moments in the living room. Upstairs she heard the toilet flush, and footsteps. She imagined Ellen washing her face, sighing at the feel of the wet washcloth against her skin, then her soft entry into the children's rooms to check on their sleep before she went to her own bed. Zoe drew a deep breath, aware of the pounding of her heart and the tingling in her hands and feet. She poured herself another whisky, neat in the glass. She tapped her foot on the floor, stood up, paced the length of the room twice. Then she heard his footfalls on the stairs; the doorknob turned and he walked into the room. He was carrying a fresh bottle of whisky and two glasses, and he was unsteady on his feet.

"Let me pour you a *real* drink."

He took the glass from her hand and set it down, wobbling, on the floor. He handed her the two empty glasses and filled the first one to the brim, the neck of the bottle swaying in his hand. He was not so successful in pouring the second drink; whisky splashed over the rim of the glass, ran down her fingers and onto the floor.

"Oh, I'm sorry."

He grabbed at her wrist in apology.

"No, it's fine."

Zoe raised her wet glass and drank from it, smiling to show him everything was all right. They were not, she realized, bad people, either of them. They could not do what they were about to do without getting drunk beforehand.

There was nothing that remained to separate them. When Douglas reached for her, when he kissed her, Zoe found that place inside herself that she had been anticipating all weekend. She found the feeling she remembered—radiant, explosive, obliterating her senses. When his arms went around her body, when his mouth closed over hers, it was like the plunger of the needle pushed home. The drug filled the cavity of her chest, flooded upwards to drown the inside of her mouth, saturated her brain.

The house stood around them, holding its breath, listening to them. The furniture itself seemed suddenly attentive, like spies sent out by Ellen to watch while she slept. Douglas lifted her sweater and touched her breasts; he drew her towards the sofa and closed his mouth over her nipple, so that she looked down upon his shorn dark curls, his bent head. The fabric covering the couch was embroidered with silken threads in a pattern of birds and blossoms; he laid her upon the cushions, knelt above her and touched her face. They were very quiet, barely whispering, both listening for his wife and his children, sleeping in their rooms above. His face leaning over hers was lined around the mouth, under the eyes, but his lips were soft. They kissed for so long that she felt herself disappear, and when he at last drew away she shook her head and pulled him closer. Zoe felt secure at last. His weight along the length of her body, his bones, his flesh, the fabric of his clothes against her clothes. She knelt in front of him and reached up beneath his shirt to find his nipples, the folds in his stomach of incipient fat. She felt the shape of his penis, stroked the length of it with her fingertips, its fevered heat, the slight jumping pulse of its response. What she felt then, what she was amazed to feel, was nothing at all, and she almost drew away. When they had stood shoulder to shoulder in front of the slaughtered animals she had felt the blood in both their bodies, an endlessly cir-culating river. But what she felt now, touching the most secret part of his body, was that they were dead. That there was nothing inside them.

It was then that they heard movement in the house. His wife, waking to use the bathroom, to check on the children? They grew still in their embrace, their lips on each other's, slightly parted, motionless. His hands were warm on her back under her sweater. He would keep holding on to her, she real-ized with amazement, he would push this moment as far as it could go. He didn't care if they were discovered, he wouldn't care about the shock and the pain on his wife's face when she turned the doorknob and opened the door and saw them together. Perhaps he needed the pain.

It was Zoe who pushed him away, scrambled off the couch. When Ellen had seen her earlier that evening, she had been wearing a dark lipstick. Now her lips were bare, blurred with kissing. The tube of lipstick was in her purse, upstairs in the spare room. If his wife walked in, there would be nothing she could say or do to conceal what had happened. She ran over to one of the lamps, switched it off, then realized it wouldn't help for Ellen to discover them in a dark room together at two in the morning, either. There was no escape. Douglas was standing in the corner, watching her. He had lit a cigarette and he was listening to his wife's footsteps upstairs. Zoe looked at him, wide-eyed, wrapping her arms around herself. He blinked and drew on his cigarette.

It was then that she knew her life was bound up with the lives of others, with actions that invited consequences. She knew this in a way she had not known when her hand had closed over Ellen's husband's penis. At any moment the door would open, Ellen would stand there outlined in lamplight, the gathered, insubstantial darkness of the hall and the staircase behind her, and she would see their eyes, the disarray of their clothing, Zoe's smeared mouth. She would see all this and her mirroring face and eyes would change.

The footsteps paused on the landing, then turned around and went back to the bedroom. There was silence once more. Zoe's arms dropped to her side. Douglas ground his cigarette clumsily into the ashtray; a plume of smoke continued to rise from the burning butt. It seemed to Zoe that there had existed an opportunity for the world to prove to her that goodness would always triumph, but nothing had happened, and she felt lost.

Douglas was the first to make a sound. He coughed, shook his head as though to clear it, came up to her and touched her arm. The shock of his wife's footsteps had sobered them both, so that they no longer looked or moved like people who had been drinking.

"We must go to bed now. You'll go to yours, and I'll go to mine."

"Will everything be all right?"

"Yes, of course. She'll be sleeping now. You go up first, I'll follow later."

In the bathroom, as Zoe washed her face and dabbed moisturizer on her cheeks, she had the curious sensation that it was to someone else's face she was ministering. The disjuncture between herself and her body seemed complete, irreparable; she did not know how to climb back inside her own skin. The face in the mirror had nothing to do with who she was, or what she had ever thought or done. She thought that all she had to do was take a step to one side, and she would physically leave her own body standing next to her.

When she left the bathroom—his razor and tufted brush on the edge of the sink, the children's jelly-coloured toothbrushes in a plastic mug, his wife's sponges and herbal soaps in a tray by the tub—she saw him standing on the landing. He was waiting for her, faceless in the dark, his shirt a pale shimmer over his body.

"Goodnight."

They kissed, his mouth open and hot on hers. The tenderness of his mouth at last opened something in her. She felt herself slide back inside her own body, felt herself fit and fill her own outline.

Only once, in the middle of the night, did she wake. Her heart was racing, and when she coughed she thought she tasted blood in the back of her throat. The formless dark increased her panic—the unfamiliar contours of the room, the distant ceiling, the ghostly high shape of the window with its drawn curtains. She thought of the man and his wife, sleeping only footsteps away, and the children who lay in their small beds. For a moment she imagined herself tiptoeing into the parents' room, easing open the door, fitting herself between their heavy, adult forms. They would each curve an arm around her and she would smell the musk of their skin and the cotton of their nightshirts, the comfort of the warm sheets and pillows, and she would sleep.

THE OUTING

SYBIL'S STOMACH CRAMPED with tension. She uncrossed her legs and tried to relax, but the chair she sat in was a modern structure of chrome bars and leather strips, and she could not get comfortable. It was the only chair in the living room of Hugh's half-furnished apartment; she was forced to wait for him with her body bent and her knees canted into the air by the angle of the seat.

This was the apartment Hugh had bought after his divorce, and Sybil saw in it a style entirely different from the one she admired in his former, shared home. In that house there was the smell of old money, a port and velvet richness to the air. The children's graduation pictures were gathered on the laquered surface of the grand piano; Lalique crystals and equine statues stood on mahogany tables; the fireplace was built up to the cathedral ceiling. Her heels sunk into the pile of the carpet in the hall.

So at first she thought that was who Hugh was—the sort of man who would always live in a house, who would not be so foolish as to leave his wife and become a bachelor in a downtown condominium. But now Hugh stood in the hall of his new apartment, knotting a tie printed with an image of Marilyn Monroe, her hair yellow as oleo, her lips parted for a kiss. Sybil watched him gazing at himself as intensely as a woman might in front of the mirrored closet door. His spiky silver moustache twitched above his lip as he smoothed the tie down upon his shirt, and as he walked towards the bathroom she saw that his hips had a feminine sashay to them. Stripped of his former surroundings, he seemed a different man from the one who had chosen her number from the escort ads in the newspaper a year ago. At their first meeting he had greeted her at the door with a cold look, poured her a crystal tumbler of Glenlivet and led her directly into the bedroom. It was her experience that most clients were nervous at first, and needed some conversation before the main event, some illusion that the encounter was more than a business transaction. His composure unsettled her. He seemed to require nothing from her beyond the sex itself, folding his clothes onto a chair and grimacing as he entered her body. It was only on subsequent visits that he let her wander through the house, and they would sit for a while afterwards in the sunken living room while he drank his Scotch. Once he let her play a tune on the grand piano, and she wondered then if he liked her, in his way.

The living room in his new apartment was uninviting in its bare, uncarpeted expanse—there was only a slab of marble servicing as a coffee table, and the white leather chair she was sitting in. This room would be cold even after he finished with it, judging by what he had done with the kitchen and the bedroom. Everything in the apartment was white or transparent, and made of something slippery—marble, chrome or glass. Sybil thought Hugh's apartment resembled something an overseas investor with too much money and no sense of style would purchase and then proceed to furnish in the modern, sleek lines he thought appealed to young women. She was surprised to discover that he no longer impressed her. He was in the bathroom, grooming his thin grey hair and checking his teeth in the mirror.

"You look really great," she said automatically when he emerged to stand at the entrance to the living room, the foyer stretching behind him so that he appeared foreshortened, like a movie star diminished by his surroundings.

"No, really?" he said with a dismissive gesture, but she could tell he was pleased. Hugh was wearing a pair of soft dress pants which draped his thick legs loosely, hiding his extra weight, and his white shirt was generously cut, bagging out at the waist. He looked like a stocky wind-up toy, comical, preposterous, a figure of fun. Sybil was forever being surprised by male vanity, which seemed to increase at middle age, in proportion to the diminishment of the attributes worthy of vanity.

"You're the one who looks fabulous," Hugh continued.

"They'll eat us up. Come on, finish your drink. It's a long drive down there and we don't want to miss anything, do we?"

He crossed over to the bar, a niche in the wall with silver, reflective shelving behind it. Expensive liqueurs were arranged on a tray, their roundish bottles like fat jewels, dark plum and murky amber. "I tell you what—let's bring a bottle with us. I have some coffee cups in the car. It'll get us in the mood."

"All right." Sybil stood up, tucking her evening bag under her arm, feeling him watch her as she crossed the living room to the foyer. The sensation was of slugs sliding over her skin. She saw him in the mirrored closet doors as he came up to her from behind, holding a bottle of Chivas by his side like a weapon with which he meant to knock her over the head. Watching him, she thought that if anyone approached them later that night, it would be because of her. They would take him only because he was part of the package, and that was why he had wanted her to go with him. He would never have made it on his own, and the knowledge of this caused her to admire herself for a moment in the mirror. Her eyes were overly bright and they flashed back at her with a desperate gleam that made her turn away from herself.

The drive down was long and would involve crossing the border, but it was only mid-afternoon when they started. The light slowly drained out of the landscape with the distance that they covered. They drove first through the city, then down a highway past several suburbs, and then all Sybil could see was farmland. At one point there was a field of horses, then a field of sheep, and then there was a stench of sulphur in the air from a nearby mill that caused Hugh to cover his nostrils.

He flipped on the radio, turning the dial from classical to pop to jazz, and then in discontent he switched it off. He didn't want to talk much, and it occurred to Sybil that this was because he didn't think she had a mind worth knowing. She chattered for a while about the books she had read recently, in an attempt to impress him, but he merely nodded and sipped from the coffee cup of Scotch he balanced between his thighs. Once in a while he put his hand on her knee and she trembled, from what she wasn't sure—surprise, disgust. But mostly he kept his eyes on the road. Sybil stared at the broad stripe of blue that was painted on the windshield to keep out the sun. The motion of the sleek, curvy car made her feel as if she was floating in a plastic bubble, adrift on water.

"Why did you leave your wife?" Sybil asked him the question that had been on her mind.

"I didn't. She left me," he said smoothly.

"Oh." Sybil was surprised. "I'm sorry. What happened? Do you miss her?"

Hugh sighed, watching the line of cars snaking through customs. "No, I don't miss her. We agreed it was for the best. She knew I was seeing other women."

Sybil couldn't think why his wife would let this end the

marriage. It was clear to her that Hugh was the sort of man whose other women—girls who worked at escort agencies, mostly—were no more individual to him than trees in a forest. She had once read a study in which nearly all the women polled said they would rather their husbands had the occasional dalliance with a prostitute than a lengthy, platonic affair of the heart with another woman. It made sense to her. She had always thought that if she married someone like Hugh, she would know enough to value the lifestyle he gave her, to consider his indiscretions a small price to be paid for the club memberships, European holidays and the stately home.

"The kids are grown up, they don't care," Hugh continued. "And I'm decorating my apartment the way I want. I can do anything I want now. It was easy."

"But you must have loved her," Sybil said.

He seemed to think about it, but then they were at the border, handing over their passports. They had tucked the bottle of Chivas away under a jacket in the back seat, and chewed a piece of Dentyne each to take the smell of it off their breaths. The man in the booth asked the ritual questions about alcohol and cigarettes, and Hugh answered him, saying he and Sybil would be back the same night. "We're just going to visit friends," he said, not blinking.

When they were on the other side, in another country, Hugh said, "No, not really."

"What?"

"No, I didn't really love her," he said. "Sybil, would you pass me the map that's in the glovebox, please?"

It was already evening, the sky massed with cloud, the air heavy and cooling. As they sped down the highway, evergreens looming on both sides, Hugh shook open the map with one hand and pinpointed their destination, muttering to himself the names of the exits up ahead. Soon they left the highway, drove through a suburb and then into a maze of back roads. Up ahead there was an abandoned factory and, opposite that, the dirt road leading to their address.

"Now, you know what to do," Hugh said as soon as they entered the parking lot. "Remember what we talked about? You know what I want. Don't disappoint me."

Then she hated him with a sharp fierceness that took her breath away. Sybil waited a minute until it passed and she was able to get out of the car. She stood next to the passenger door, shaking out her legs and looking around her. There were vehicles of every make in the parking lot, from family sedans to candy-coloured two-seaters, rusty Hondas to Mercedes and BMWs. At the far end of the lot there was a chain-link fence and a gate, and beyond that a glimpse of greenery and a building that would be the club. It was dark and there wasn't much she could see beyond the wall of trees, and suddenly she felt entirely conspicuous, and watched, as though someone in the club was observing them with a camera. Hugh's face creased in an unfamiliar expression of worried excitement, and he held out his hand for her to take. She moved towards him; the oystery silk blouse she had chosen to wear felt aglow against her skin, rendering her an easy target in the night.

Someone must have been watching them arrive after all, because they were met at the gate by a corpulent woman in an ankle-length skirt printed with daisies. Her cheeks were lustily red in a way that might have seemed an indication of health in another, thinner person, but in her it seemed a sign of disease.

"Hello, I'm Mabel," she said, wiping strands of corn-coloured hair off her forehead. Her voice was surprisingly light, musical. "Welcome. I haven't seen either of you here before. Is this your first time? Are your names on our list?"

"Yes," Hugh said to both questions. He let go of Sybil's hand and reached into his pocket for a slip of paper, which he passed to Mabel. "That's our confirmation number. The fee is already looked after."

Mabel checked the numbers against a list attached to a clipboard she had been holding against her thigh. "Paul Smithers and Julie Campbell?"

"That's us," Hugh and Sybil said simultaneously, too quickly.

Mabel looked from one to the other, her eyes narrowing in knowing amusement. Sybil could feel the heat rising to her face under the other woman's scrutiny.

"Follow me, then. I'll show you into the dining hall, a number of our guests are having dinner there right now, so you'll have a chance to meet them first. The meal's nothing fancy, roast chicken, salad and potatoes, but I'm assuming you didn't come for the food."

Sybil laughed along with her, shamefully. She could feel the muscles of her shoulders tense, and she made shrugging movements under her blouse to try to loosen them. In the night, the evergreens around them pressing in with a greater darkness, she heard Hugh's slightly asthmatic breathing beside her, and for the first time smelled the lingering chemical odour of his cologne. They walked past a formal garden with paths that glowed faintly through the grass, and several flower beds, and statuary posed in classical positions, before arriving at the club.

Mabel left them at the entrance to the dining hall—"Enjoy yourselves, I have to look in on the others, I'll be looking in on you later tonight!"—and they went in and seated themselves at an empty table. The hall was high-ceilinged, with a stage and a space for dancing, and a set of French doors opening onto a terrace with wrought-iron tables and little white chairs—like those used for tea parties in period movies, Sybil thought. There were at least fifty people in the hall, most of them couples except for several men in their twenties who were alone.

Hugh and Sybil filled their plates at the buffet table and returned to their seats, picking at their food, searching the room for someone special. The other couples in the hall did the same.

"Well, this is nice," Hugh said, half-whispering. "Isn't this nice?"

"Yes, the food is really good," Sybil said to provoke him.

"Look around you," he hissed. "Come on, smile at someone you like. Remember what I want you to do."

A flush of rage rose in her chest, reminding her in its strength and impulse of adolescent rages. But she had agreed to come tonight and, of course, he had given her a sum of money for her trouble. The money was like a contract between them, binding; she would do what she had been paid to do, regardless of how aware she was that it was possible for her to do nothing, to pick up her purse and turn and walk out of the hall with fifty pairs of eyes watching her. It was true she would not have come if Hugh weren't paying her, but there was more to it than that. His world had been one she had always wanted for herself— when she used to visit him in his house while his wife was away, she would pretend that what she saw there belonged to her. She would walk through the house as if it were hers, trailing her fingers along the fine surfaces, imagining how only the night before she had been a gracious host to her guests around the crystal-laden dining-room table, or how she must now select a gown to wear at tonight's gala fund-raiser from the dozens that hung in rustling folds in her very own dressing room. But now everything was changed, and Sybil could not think of a single fantasy to get her through this night.

"Well, who do you see?"

"That couple over there, near the buffet table. They seem attractive to me."

The man had sandy blond hair, he was slim and wore a pin-striped shirt. He was like most of the other men in the hall, ordinary, a few of them verging on good-looking. Sybil imagined that the men in their twenties would have appeared handsome in a different context, seen on a sunny downtown street in the middle of summer perhaps, with strands of their hair bleached from idle afternoons rollerblading or surfing. Here she could only associate them with pornographic magazines, stale rooms with unwashed sheets and underwear on the floor, masturbation.

The man's partner was beautiful in a way none of the other women were. She was tall and curvy and wore a close-fitting minidress printed with blue flowers. She had wavy auburn hair that fell to her shoulders, and her features were marred only by the thick pink lipstick that coated her mouth. She looked back at Sybil and Hugh, and after a while turned and bent her head, whispering something to the man beside her. He nodded, and they both stood up and walked towards Sybil's table. Around them people were finishing their meals, sitting back and sipping wine, or starting to leave the room in a self-conscious manner, aware that everyone else knew where they were going. Some of the couples had started to talk to each other in low voices further obscured by the music issuing from the speakers at the foot of the stage, early-eighties tunes Sybil recognized from her adolescence.

"Hi. My name's Angela and this is Richard. Mind if we join you?"

They shook hands and the other couple sat down. Out of the corner of her eye Sybil saw Hugh looking the other woman up and down and smiling to himself in a self-congratulatory manner. The two men began to talk right away, and Sybil turned politely to the woman.

"Where are you from? Are you two married?"

"Oh, we're from around here. Richard's my fiancé, we're getting married in a month. It's very exciting." Angela toyed with a silver bracelet on her wrist; her nails were long and painted the same opaque pink as her lips. "We met at work, actually— he's a lawyer, and I'm a paralegal. What about you two?"

"I'm studying science in university, Paul is a marine biologist. We're just dating." All of it was lies, rehearsed beforehand back in the apartment, and she saw by the way Angela looked at her, shifted her gaze to include Hugh, and then looked briefly away, that she knew it was a lie, too. But what wouldn't be, in a place like this? Sybil wondered. How likely was it that the man Angela was with was a lawyer, as opposed to—what? A veterinarian, a clerk in a grocery store, an insurance adjuster? What did all these details matter here, when anonymity was the only thing that could make this evening possible? Next to her, as if sensing a slippage in the role they had created for themselves, Hugh reached over and grasped Sybil's hand proprietorially, linking his fingers among hers. Angela and Richard, following suit, leaned over and kissed each other; Angela laid a hand on the side of his face and whispered into his ear.

"We like you," she said to Sybil and Hugh when she pulled away. "But we're going to walk around the club for a bit. We've been here a few times before, and I bet there's some people we know already here. We'll meet up later in one of the rooms, all right?"

"Sure, yes. We'll do that," Hugh said for the both of them, somewhat too eagerly. And then they were left alone. The music had been turned up, and the more exhibitionistic couples were dancing at the foot of the stage. Their movements were awkward, full of the knowledge that their bodies were being examined and either lusted after or rejected by those who were watching.

Perhaps it was the Scotch in the car on the way down, and then the wine at dinner; perhaps it was how much she did not want to be there—whatever the reason, Sybil already felt the evening beginning to blur. The club was enormous, a sprawling wooden star with dozens of corridors which led to bedrooms, saunas and low-ceilinged attics with mattresses on the floor. A few of the rooms were so vast they held half a dozen queen-sized beds. There was even a screening room, where couples reclined on blocks of foam, watching giant images projected across one wall.

Sybil found herself in the change room next to the pool, where several women with wet hair padded about in towels and bare feet. They smiled at Sybil, who left her clothes in a locker and walked out naked to the blue, undisturbed rectangle of the pool. She slipped in and began to swim in short, clumsy strokes; soon she rolled over onto her back and paddled her feet, gazing up at the fluorescent lights and wooden beams crossing the ceiling above, hearing the sound of her own breath distorted by water and space. It was harsh and enormously hollow to her ears. She was aware she had just finished eating and that she had had a lot to drink, and she thought maliciously that it would serve Hugh right if she were to swallow water and drown. What would he do? What would he tell his ex-wife, his daughter who was not much younger than Sybil herself? His daughter with the brassy blonde hair and blue eyes, who wore tennis clothes and mugged for the camera in one of the photographs on the grand piano.

Lying on the surface of the pool, a skin of water lapping over her legs and belly, Sybil fantasized about Hugh's long, frantic drive home. Who would he call first? How would he explain what had happened? She smiled at the thought of the panic that would crumple his features. Such a small man, how would he ever cope with a scandal like that?

When she heard the splash of another person in the pool she swam for the ladder leading up the side. Before she could climb up another woman grabbed her hand and hoisted her out of the water. This other woman had cropped brown hair and long, ponderous breasts, and she patted Sybil on the rear with a boastful laugh. Her eyes were as aggressive as any man's. Sybil pulled away and ran to the change room, the tiles underfoot so hard they seemed to slap up at her bare feet.

She towelled herself off hurriedly in front of the lockers, turning her back to the naked women padding in and out of the showers. What she wanted to do was wrap herself in something concealing, a coat or a blanket, but instead she reached into her bag for the outfit she knew Hugh would like—a lacy red teddy and high heels. It made her feel more naked than if she was wearing nothing at all, but she knew she looked good, and that others would want her.

She breathed deeply and walked out into the club. The hallways were lit with red and blue bulbs, the colour they shed thickening the air and somehow the senses. The colours had a slowing, deadening effect on her brain, like drugs; they weighed her limbs down. She felt she was moving through fog, as in a dream. But it was not late enough for her to be dreaming. What was it—maybe ten o'clock, eleven at most. Outside the grass would be crunchy with moisture, and the sky would not yet have reached the complete, absolving dark of midnight.

"This place is amazing," Hugh whispered when they found each other. Together they walked in and out of rooms filled with naked bodies in couples, threesomes and groups. The air around them smelled of ripe wood, sweat and saline. "Just incredible." He pulled Sybil along with him, holding not her hand but rather her wrist. Occasionally a naked body would emerge from the shadows and squeeze past Hugh and Sybil, giggling, and sometimes a man or a woman would reach out and put a hand on Sybil's breast, or touch her hair, or kiss her, while Hugh watched. She could sense his hunger, his greed, like electricity crackling beside her.

He chose a room, and pushed her down onto a mattress. Around her the air was filled with whispers and moans; there was the occasional shout or crescendoing scream, followed by embarrassed laughter. Hugh watched as another man approached Sybil. The man was in his twenties, with curly hair and wearing what must have been uncomfortably tight white jeans which glowed in the light of the coloured bulbs. She looked at him through half-closed eyes. He seemed young to her, compared to the men whose homes or hotel rooms she visited, and she hoped he would not be too rough or eager. Hugh kept prodding her shoulder while the man had sex with her; he whispered jealous, accusatory words in her ear and yet he would not allow her to stop having sex with the stranger, who panted rhythmically against the side of her neck. Sybil could see past him towards the mirrored wall, see that his legs were long and pale, the trunks of saplings. She could also see Hugh on his knees beside them, masturbating in a regular, practised motion.

At some point the stranger finished, kissed her for the first time on the mouth, and said, "Thank you." Then he pulled on his white jeans and left the room, and she watched him go. She thought that she would not recognize him if she saw him in full daylight, that she did not even know his name. After three years of working as an escort she was still amazed by this. It had been so simple, so forgettable.

"I bet you loved it, didn't you?" Hugh hissed into her face, his breath hotter than the close room. He had let go of his penis without ejaculating, and now it bobbed anxiously in the air. "I bet you just loved his big cock inside you. Tell me what it was like, having his big, thick cock inside you?"

Sybil summoned a smile. She thought how angry he would be if she told him the truth—that she had detached from herself so completely that she had not felt a thing. "I loved it, yes."

Sybil and Hugh continued to wander from room to room, his tie now wadded into a trouser pocket, Sybil with only a towel around her body. They were propositioned, fondled, invited to join this couple or that group, but they declined with a smile and a shake of the head. Once they saw Mabel, huge in her daisy-printed skirt, standing in the doorway of one of the rooms like a mother checking on her sleeping brood.

It was in a downstairs room, not far from the swimming pool—Sybil could smell the chlorine leaching the air, hear the faint susurration of water, the pool's high-ceilinged echoes and amplifications—that they found Angela and Richard, the couple they had met in the dining hall. They were entangled on a king-sized bed, kissing and murmuring to each other; Angela's engagement ring flashed in the lamplight. She saw Sybil and Hugh over the curve of her fiancé's shoulder, and instantly waved them over.

"Isn't she lovely?" Richard said, patting his girlfriend's thigh. Angela laughed softly and twined her fingers through his. "And yours—what a beauty." He placed his free hand on one of Sybil's breasts, turning the nipple between his fingers. She thrust out her chest for him to admire; her body felt numb, and for a moment she imagined she was only a mannequin, made of plaster, with a hollow, airy centre.

"Yes, they're a sight, aren't they?" Hugh was hastily removing his clothes, his eyes scanning back and forth. He seemed torn between the sight of the two naked women and the vision of Richard's slim, erect penis standing against his taut stomach. "Look at Syb—I mean, Julie's breasts. They're beautiful. And your girl—she's so pretty. The two of them together, look at their cunts."

"My Angel has the hottest cunt, like warm butter sliding over your cock. Oh, I'd love to see her with your girl, it would be incredible. Honey?" he said to Angela, who had already put her hands on Sybil's breasts, and was kissing her belly. "Do you like her?" He had one hand on his penis, stroking.

"Oh, yes," Angela said, and awkwardly positioned herself between Sybil's thighs. Her tongue on Sybil's clitoris felt warm and rough, smaller and more pointed than a man's tongue. It was at once more knowing yet shy, licking and then flickering aside, hesitating, buying time; then another small, dragging lick, and a fumbling kiss, and then a caress with her hair full and spread out between Sybil's thighs. It was so odd, Sybil thought—this woman's pretty face with her youthful chin and the pink lipstick that had smeared all over her mouth, lying between Sybil's thighs as if she were a man. Sybil heard Hugh say, embarrassment colouring his voice, "May I?" and Richard laughing and saying, "Sure." She turned her head, opened her eyes and saw Hugh clumsily kneeling to take the other man's penis in his mouth. He held the first few inches between his lips and began to suck, but Richard's pelvic movements popped the penis out of his mouth so that he had to struggle to keep it, his seeking, directionless face full of vulnerability, of the pain of wanting what kept eluding his grasp.

THE SUMMER PLACE

On her way to the island, Catherine saw a fishing boat in the middle of the ocean, on fire. The pilot saw it at the same time, a curlicue of charcoal smoke winding upwards in the expanse of blue. Their plane was still miles away, and other than the smoke there was only water and sky. They were alone in the four-passenger aircraft, heavy avocado-coloured earmuffs clamped to their heads. Silent but for the crackling exchanges over the radio. Once when Catherine unlatched the window it sprang open violently, sucked out by the wind, and then it was so noisy in the plane she could not think.

The pilot radioed in that he was diverting from the flight path in order to investigate the source of the smoke. They flew lower, and various gauges ticked back and forth on the controls. They were still five miles away from the boat, and as they approached the whisker of smoke grew to a column, pouring upwards into the sky, with an orange rose at its base. The smoke whirled and spun at its edges, and the rose blossomed into flames.

It was a salmon fishing boat, consumed by fire from stem to stern. Flames danced on its deck as the plane circled lower and lower. Now Catherine could smell the ash and feel the heat scorching the wind. This close the sea dwindled; there was only the fire, sheets of neon lashing the sky.

Help was already coming, in the form of two white boats carving paths through the water towards the fire. It was then that she saw there was someone to be saved—an orange dot in the water was a life buoy, with a pair of white arms waving up at the blue plate of the sky, the burning sun and their plane.

Catherine felt she did not want this moment to end, the astonishing beauty of fire in the middle of the sea. She wished for her camera; she had left it behind because it signified work, and the week ahead was supposed to be a holiday. She wanted to capture the sight, to put her hands up to her face, square off the image between them, to squint and see.

When one of the two boats was only heartbeats away from the floating man, the pilot radioed in that the coast guard was on its way, and he would be resuming his original course. They spun away from the flames faster than they had descended, veering away in a smooth arc. In an instant, the drama was behind them. Far ahead lay the green island, with a patch of yellow that was Max's land, his summer place.

Catherine met Barry several months ago when she had taken his photograph for a business magazine. He was one of the directors of a holding company downtown; the company had recently enjoyed an upswing, and the partners were being profiled that month. Their offices were on the eighteenth floor of one of those hushed, luxurious high-rises, all indirect lighting, mirrored elevators and floral arrangements, that were like five-star hotels. Glass doors to their reception area whispered open, revealing marble floors, silk-covered sofas, sculptures. The art on the walls was by a famous local painter who had made his millions from nouveau-riche players in penny stocks who filled their houses with his work. Cold bays, sloping rocks, water and sky washing together in arctic colours. Catherine, waiting with her equipment, looked at the paintings and wondered what it would be like to be so successful an artist. She didn't want that for herself, at least not any more. Photography was a job, though years ago she had striven for more—displaying black-and-white prints in rundown galleries, of faces turned away, nude bodies drifting under bathwater. Somewhere along the way she lost the art student's hunger; perhaps it was during her relationship with Peter, the way they had always competed, his art, hers, the way he always won. Whenever a critic acknowledged her talent, whenever she made a sale or had a higher attendance at her openings, life with him became a lot more difficult. It was easier, in the end, to withdraw. The business magazines paid well for their stiff portraits of directors and executives, one leg angled up on their chairs, grimacing gamely.

Catherine had not been attracted to Barry, but his attraction towards her, the laser gaze of his interest, was enough at the time. He was shorter than her, stocky, with a full face and narrow eyes that reflected light like glaciers. Catherine could not quite figure him out. He seemed bright, with a variety of interests, but lacked the spark she had come to associate with men in business—a certain hardness, a keen ability to manipulate. Barry seemed, well, nice. Scrubbed and polite. He said "please" and "thank you" and spoke highly of other men in business, whom Catherine in her dealings with them knew to be unpleasant.

They went out on several dates, dinners and plays and classical music concerts. He drove a Rolls-Royce, boxy as a refrigerator, and wore designer clothes with the labels stitched on the pockets. His hands, when he touched her on the arm or gave her an impromptu neck massage, were the softest she had ever encountered, as though he had not done a day's work in his life. Catherine imagined him retiring at night with his hands gloved in Vaseline.

They had yet to progress beyond a kiss goodnight. Then Barry invited her to come with him to Max's summer home on the island. There would be other guests there, and long dinners sparkling with conversation. Many of the city's business elite had property on the island, and they all knew each other. He promised her an interesting time and so she agreed to go. She did not want to dwell on the failure of her relationship with Peter. And she was curious about Barry's world. He knew Max from business dealings; it seemed all the investors in the city had dealt with each other at some point, their partnerships forming and breaking apart like marriages. It was a world that was mysterious to her, beyond the reach of her photographs. She never understood the accompanying articles—business, it seemed, had its own language and lexicon. Editors of magazines and newspapers called her, she took photographs, they were published. That was concrete. Money was fairly concrete, too, but stocks were something she had never owned and did not understand. So the lives of these men were mysterious to her. They got up early to make phone calls to other countries, that was all she really knew. The rest was paperwork and meetings, and reading the financial sections of half a dozen newspapers every day.

What she knew of Max was that he was one of the most successful men in the city. He had made his money from the sale of one of his companies—something unglamorous, dog food or carpet-cleaning supplies. Whatever it was had made him a millionaire, and he still had his finger in other pies, interests in at least a dozen other companies. She knew that he collected acquaintances the way other people might collect butterfly specimens or stamps. She had met him once at a hospital fundraiser where she was taking photographs for the society page of a magazine. It was held in a closed wing of the hospital; there were tables labelled "Dermatology," "Urology," "Pathology," seated by doctors who had collectively given ten thousand dollars in donations. Max was working the room, business cards and Post-it notes at hand, saying hello to his friends who were investment analysts, senior partners of law firms, honorary consuls.

When Catherine told Barry that she wanted separate bedrooms he had cheerfully said yes, of course, he wasn't bringing her so that they could be a couple. She was relieved; all she wanted from him was a distraction from the ruins of her last relationship, a social schedule to fill her evenings. She didn't know what he wanted from her. Perhaps it was companionship. She'd heard that with men his age it wasn't about sex, but companionship. So she said yes. He went up several days earlier—she had a last-minute newspaper assignment—and she followed, in the plane that Max chartered for her.

"Welcome!" Barry cried, throwing his arms open to include the house as he led her through the living room to the deck. He beamed as though it were his, and he was offering it to her. She glimpsed a symphony of colour and textured-leather furniture, wood floors, the hewn black oak of the dining-room table. There were paintings, sculptures, pottery and blankets everywhere, unmistakably arranged by a designer. Then they were out on the deck, overlooking acreage. The hayfield was like cream in the sunlight, and went on and on. There were evergreens at the edges of the property, and in the distance the water wearing its coat of diamonds.

The air was warm, lazy, honey-thick. A mosquito buzzed and she scratched at her bare elbow. The silence was like molasses slowly pouring out of a jug.

"There's more oxygen up here," Barry said, settling next to her on the wicker sofa. "You'll find you'll sleep better here. You'll get up later and later each morning. I guarantee it."

Catherine had always thought of oxygen-rich air as sharp and invigorating, not this mellow, beery richness, not air with a texture to it, and a clinging perfume from the hanging flower baskets.

There was a commotion at the front of the house, footsteps, and Max came through the French doors onto the deck. He was wearing tennis whites, and drew his left wrist, wrapped in a sweatband, across his forehead. "Catherine, Catherine," he said, smiling with pleasure. She rose to shake his hand, but he opened his arms and drew her in. When he bent to plant a kiss on the top of her head, his chin bumped her forehead, flustering her. He smelled good, manly, and she noticed this more than she wanted to. "Welcome. I'm so glad Barry invited you. How was your flight?"

She began to tell him about the boat burning in the middle of the blue water. He pulled over a chair from the breakfast table and sat down. Light glinted on the blond hairs of his long legs. He had thick white hair that lay plastered sweatily on his scalp. His hands were gigantic, and his head seemed twice the size of hers.

Then his girlfriend, back from her tennis lesson, was in the doorway. Tiny, barely five feet, with the thin legs and delicate frame of a child, she was half Max's age, with ivory skin, platinum hair and extraordinary eyes—marble green, flecked with gold. She was not perspiring, and did not look as if she ever did.

"You must be Catherine," Claire said, extending her hand. It was cool against Catherine's, the fingers sliding along hers, not grasping.

Barry wanted to go down to the beach for a swim. He lifted Catherine's bags and headed across the yard to the cabin where she would sleep; his own room was in the main house. She followed his short, thick stride; his city clothes had concealed how plump, and solid, he really was. He had not shaved, and this gave his full face and sharp eyes a rather wild look.

The cabin was surrounded with larkspur and phlox, where fat bumblebees hung, nudging the blossoms, their nearly circular striped bodies idly buzzing. The door banged open to reveal a long, rectangular space with a bathroom in the corner, two queen-sized beds and a large living area. Framed posters from philanthropic events decorated the log walls. While Barry paced the room, fussing with the blinds, hanging a mosquito net over the bed she had chosen, she wandered over to the bookshelf and pulled out several volumes.

"Oh, Max loves to read. Even short stories and poems," Barry said in a rather puzzled voice. The books in Barry's house were non-fiction hardcovers, biographies of national pollsters and chairmen of multinational banks, business books on East-West investments and entrepôt capital markets. The books in the cabin were all contemporary literary titles, except for several thick hardcovers on men's health and the aging male body.

Catherine went into the bathroom to arrange her toiletries on a wooden shelf. When she glanced in the mirror above the sink she realized she could only see the top half of her face. She was nearly six feet tall, but Max was taller, and he had hung all the mirrors in the cabin at his own height.

The beach was accessed by walking the length of the hayfield, then down a rocky slope to the water. She went with Barry, who carried their towels; Max and Claire had gone ahead to change into their bathing suits on the beach, while she and Barry had changed in their rooms. The tall grass scratched her legs. Along the way they passed a herd of Max's cows, great placid animals with yellow tags drooping from their ears.

"Do you like cows?" Barry asked.

"Well, I've never met one before, so I wouldn't know," she said. It was the plain truth, but he laughed so uproarously that she felt momentarily bright and immensely witty. The fact was, she was overwhelmed—it was the first time she had been outside the city, and there was something electric about Max that disturbed her slightly. The germ of an infatuation, growing inside her. Ahead of her was a week with strangers, and only Barry, whom she barely knew, to guide her and protect her. Nature was all around, and she wasn't sure she was comfortable with it. Already, as they walked across the field, she was starting to sneeze allergically.

Max and Claire were already in the water, swimming far out. Barry took her hand and helped her negotiate her way to the shore along flat, circular shapes of sloping rock that were warm and porous beneath her feet. When she took off her cover-up she winced, feeling not only the sun along her body but Barry's sideways appraisal.

"Come on, the water's lovely. That looks like a good place to enter," Barry called from the rock he had clambered upon. "Watch out for the barnacles, and the seaweed, it's slippery!"

The seaweed waved back and forth, damp olive, under the water, and there was a bewilderment of rocks studded with barnacles. Catherine picked her way carefully to the edge, planting her feet here and there. The water was warm, itself slippery. A cluster of barnacles jabbed at the soles of her feet. As she stepped on the seaweed it skidded out from under her, pliant as a sheet of wet plastic, and the shallow water suddenly, inexplicably deepened. She fell hard.

"Are you all right?" Barry called.

"Yeah," she mumbled, scrambling to stay on the surface, the

earth beneath having slipped away. She held her palms up to the sun and watched them bleed. The barnacles had acted like razors, slicing thin, sharp lines that were starting to burn. One of her heels was torn as well, bleeding into the blue water, which was viscous with salt. She splashed, treading water, trying to laugh. "Yeah, I'm fine."

Barry was next to her, whooping, laughing. His grey hair, wet, looked thin. "You're always falling around me, why is that?"

It was true. On their first date, climbing up the winding stairs to the boxy shape of the Rolls-Royce in the one a.m. darkness, only the faintest trace of moonlight to illuminate her path, she had missed the curved platform of the top step and turned her ankle, falling partway back down the stairs. It was a funny feeling, falling, like tumbling weightless through space, and in that moment she had wanted to land on the cement bottom, to let go of life. Her relationship with Peter was finally, miserably over, and she was tired of everything. Her limbs folded over each other in a comfortable tangle, and while she was falling she thought, from some detached place outside herself, Well, it doesn't matter anyway. But then to her own disappointment, independently of her mind, her hands and knees shot out and gained purchase on the steps, and held on.

"Yes, I'm always falling," she acquiesced, and then Max was nearby, his face like a rock sculpture, his shoulders powerful, his hair dripping water down his cheeks. He said, "What's that? You're always falling in love, did you say?"

"No," she said, clumsily treading water, "no." Claire was swimming towards them, slender and lithe, her body slicing through the water like a penknife.

"Claire's half fish," Barry murmured. The two men watched Catherine as she turned and paddled a short distance away from them. The water was like sheets of satin brushing her body. She was not far out, but already she did not know where the bottom of the ocean lay. When she gazed out at what she thought was the horizon, the soft blue sky washed over the water and gave her vertigo—there was no point of reference, no dividing line between earth and sky and the universe—so that she had to turn, gasping, back to the sight of her three companions, their solid bodies and faces in the water as real then as land.

Later, as they picked their way back to their clothes and towels on the beach, Catherine hobbling to favour her cut heel, Max knelt down and beckoned her beside him. "Look at this. This is a whole other world," he said, pointing to a stream of water where life forms lived, tiny snails and bristling anemones and what looked like wriggling fingernail parings. He selected one of the larger anemones, pink with gelatinous tentacles waving back and forth, and touched it with a fingertip. "If you do that, it'll close around you."

And so it did, around her forefinger, the small earnest mouth of this tiny creature suckling her flesh.

That evening there were cocktails and dinner out on the deck, with guests arriving from around the island. Barry made the rounds with a bottle of wine and a napkin over his left arm; earlier he had bent close to Catherine and sprayed her exposed skin with Off! to repel the mosquitoes that would devour them as they sat down to dinner.

Inside the vast kitchen—an expanse of shining copper pots and pans, the sweep of a granite counter, all the silver surfaces polished to a gunmetal gleam—the cook was preparing dinner. Claire was greeting the arriving guests, touching them on the arm, steering them out onto the deck. Max came out wearing jeans and a colourful striped shirt that made Catherine think of blocks of Lego. When she told him this, he glanced at her and said, "Lego? Hmm. Maybe you should put me together." She did not know what to say then, and directed her attention to the two ducks that had wandered onto the deck. Max scooped one of them up in his arms, where it wrestled against his embrace, and brought it close to her so she could reach out and touch its red face. The bumpy, alarmingly warm red flesh felt, she said, like the neck of an old man, and he laughed at that and let the duck go.

Catherine let her glass be refilled again. The chatter around her grew louder, and the air felt friendlier. The dinner guests were doctors and business executives in their city lives, but here they appeared like countrymen in rumpled shirtsleeves and sandals. Their wives were artistically inclined, writing poetry or painting watercolours. They wore peasant blouses, billowing cotton skirts, and dangling earrings they themselves had fashioned out of wire and seashells. They looked young, like girls, but with lines around their eyes and well-cut silver hair.

Catherine was seated opposite Max at the hewn wooden table where they ate on the deck. Claire, to his left, appeared tiny next to him, a small bird with slender, darting fingers. It had grown dark, and now the flames of the candles swept low, blowing horizontal, then out. Barry went into the house and emerged with a pair of what looked like birdcages, with votive candles burning steadily inside them. Still she could hardly make out the shapes of her food in the dark. It was the faces that were bright, and the gleam of jewellery. Max watched her carefully whenever she spoke, as though he were trying to figure her out.

The conversation somehow turned to detachment. One of the wives, who was in the middle of writing a novel, said that she had always felt herself to be outside of any situation, an observer rather than a participant, even of her own emotions. "Maybe that's what being a writer is all about," she said with a flourish of ringed fingers.

"Oh, I don't think so," a psychiatrist said, shaking his head. A button under his navel was undone, lending him the look of a man who had just tumbled out of his house after a day of watching television and drinking beer. But his face was stern and his hair a crisp halo of white. "I don't think it's just writers.

I'm detached." He turned to Catherine; his eyes were almond-shaped and utterly opaque. "Most of my friends can be detached. Wouldn't you say that's true? What about you and your photography?"

"Oh, I am too," Catherine said, and all around her there were nods and echoes from the other guests: "Yes, me too, I'm detached." Max simply watched her, not moving. "But I'm not really an artist," she added. "I just take pictures for a living."

Later, when dessert and coffee were served, she looked at Max and said brazenly, a bit drunkenly, "Looking at you makes me happy."

Catherine woke early, and through the film of the mosquito net saw the sky and water beyond the cabin window pink with the rising sun. It was like a postcard. There was noise outside—geese, perhaps. The spill of the finely meshed net was like a bride's veil around her. She felt safe and went back to sleep, not wanting to think about anything.

The days on the island, she quickly discerned, were a roundelay of idle activities: tennis, badminton, hikes around Max's sprawling property, swims twice a day. In the mornings, Max, Claire and Barry disappeared for a three-hour game of tennis before the sun rose too high in the sky, and Catherine wandered around the property alone. Perched on a stool in the kitchen to talk to the cook, she would make herself a breakfast of fried eggs from the fresh ones that Max brought in still warm, snugged in a basket. Sometimes the eggs were huge, and these spilled forth double yolks, twin orange suns collapsing onto the sizzling pan.

They seemed born to their games, these people. When they came back from tennis they were exhausted but exuberant, and ready for a dip in the cool ocean. During the day they lived on handfuls of granola, yoghurt and strawberries spooned out of blue ceramic bowls, pitchers of juice and ice water. Catherine wondered when Max and Claire had time for each other, when Max had time for his books. When they were not playing games or entertaining guests, he was herding the cows, gathering the eggs, or on the phone to his executive assistant in the city, speaking a foreign language of stocks and mergers.

One afternoon, reluctant to return to the salt water when her palms were still slit open, Catherine sat on the porch with a sketchpad while the others went for a swim. Max, Claire and Barry walked away from her down the hayfield, colourful striped towels slung over their shoulders, talking animatedly. She drew their outlines on the page, three distinct figures in a vast field—Max tall and powerfully built, Barry short and rectangular, Claire tucked between them. Max's head was inclined towards his girlfriend, and he appeared to be listening intently to everything she was saying.

Then Catherine sketched herself into the picture, in the space on Max's other side, her own long body striding next to his. She frowned down at the page. If anything, she and Max were too well matched. Their figures seemed to tower over Claire's and Barry's. She drew Max holding her hand, as though they were a couple, but when she next looked up she saw that it was Claire's hand he was holding, Claire who was small and delicate and in need of protection.

Later Max returned by himself. Catherine laid her sketchbook face down next to her and squinted, watching him come across the field. He had the easy, rolling stride of someone comfortable in his body, indeed, pleased by it. She watched in admiration, and with a faint ache.

Claire was the one Catherine saw least. She was always going shopping, looking for new pottery or paintings in the studios of the many artists on the island, or for a massage that took two hours, from which she returned with a dazed expression and slower gestures. When she was in the house she often pulled Barry aside and wanted to talk to him, show him the greeting cards or homemade candles she had just bought. He was like her brother, Catherine saw, she trusted him. Was he trustworthy, then?

Barry thrived here, although he complained about the occasional phone call that necessitated a trip with the cordless out to the deck where he paced. "It's a business call," he'd say, returning. "Terrible. I can't relax. Business." He was never more explicit than that.

But he took responsibility for Catherine. When she went to the cabin to read, or nap, half-conscious of the voices and laughter carrying across the yard from the main house, often she would look up to see him on tiptoe, his face at the window of her door, knocking gently and hoping to be let in. He took her for drives around the island, which all looked the same to her, evergreens and the glimmer of water in the distance. The shops at the centre of town sold tie-dyed shirts and organic groceries and pricey carvings and jewellery to the tourists and the well-to-do city folk whose summer homes were here. The locals were stuck in a time warp—they wore flowing cotton clothes, no make-up and sandals in the midday heat.

Day by day, Barry touched her more frequently. He would seize her by the waist, plant kisses on her cheeks, give her neck massages and close hugs. Then, as though to prove he wasn't singling her out, he would grab Claire, or the cook, to rumple their hair, to pinch them till they laughed and sprang away from him. Catherine relaxed into it. They were all like that, generous with their affection, though one night when Max asked her for a hug while she was helping with dinner in the kitchen, she stood uneasily against his embrace, his warmth, his good smell.

Barry took her for a walk along the edge of the property, into the evergreens. They were in their swimsuits, headed down for the beach. "See that over there?" he said, pointing at an enclosed paddock. "It's empty now, Claire doesn't ride. Max built it for his previous wife, for dressage."

"Did she use it much?"

"I'm not sure she used it at all." He sighed. "That's Max though, always trying to please his women."

The navy water rippled below the cliffs ahead. They were walking in overgrown brush and were forced to negotiate every step, avoiding brambles, stomping down patches of thick weeds. The long grasses came up past Catherine's knees, and she felt a flash of annoyance towards Barry when they scratched her skin. Once he held back a branch to let her pass, brushing her breast with his hand as she did so; she took the branch from him but let it snap back at him when he followed. She knew then that her feelings for him would never change into love.

Max and Claire were sitting in the shade of a sloping rock on the beach, their bare legs stretched out in front of them. He was applying antiseptic to a cut on her elbow. Catherine saw that it was his role to take care of her, and she recalled how tenderly he had covered Claire's hand at dinner the night before, saying, "I didn't use to have white hair. I didn't have Claire to worry about then." Claire, next to him, had looked like a tiny child, and Catherine realized that Max considered his position in his girlfriend's life to be precarious, and that it was the first time in his charmed life that a woman had not loved him more than he loved her.

The sun was deceptively soft on their skin; the water was too cold to go swimming. Catherine noticed a gash of red on Max's calf and pointed. Dark red blood had congealed to a trickle. "You cut yourself."

He turned to regard the back of his calf dispassionately. "Oh, so I have. Look at that. Wait, you know what it is?" He touched the red with a fingertip, brought it to his lips. Sugar, red seeds. "It's raspberry jam." He smiled, squinting up at Catherine. Beside him Claire studied her elbow and pouted, angling it towards him for further ministrations. She was wearing a bikini which she did not quite fill out. Sand lay over their bodies like a layer of brown sugar. The water was a crisp blue sheet ignited by the sun. When Catherine sat on a nearby rock, bringing her legs up to her chin, she smelled salt on her warm limbs. Barry was out in the chill water, up to his thighs in it, one hand shielding his eyes as he gazed out to a sailboat on the horizon. The tide was high. Catherine saw that Max did not need anyone to look after him, did not need anyone to put him together.

Max and Claire were having several friends over for dinner one evening, then a party afterwards to which they had invited everyone they knew on the island. Earlier in the day Catherine and Barry accompanied them into town to help them shop for food and wine; they took Max's Landrover, Claire and Max sitting in the back, his hand eclipsing her thigh. On the ride home, their groceries in the back, Max bent to kiss her and she pulled away from him, laughing.

"My friends who've met Max say, 'Watch out, that man is a lover.' He loves women, don't you, Max?"

"Oh, I'm a lover, am I?" He settled back into the seat and grinned at Catherine, who had turned to watch them. "But those days are behind me now."

They turned down the long driveway, thick with evergreens on both sides, to Max's house. The two men carried the groceries through the open front door to the kitchen while Claire and Catherine unloaded them from the trunk of the car. Claire gazed at her partner, his broad shoulders moving under his shirt as he hoisted three bulging paper sacks.

"Once when I was a girl, my sister and I visited a psychic," Claire mused. "We wanted to know about our futures with men, of course, and the psychic told us that we were two different types of women. She was the sort of woman that men marry, and I was the sort that men have affairs with. Imagine!" She laughed. "But it's turned out totally opposite. I'm the sort that men marry."

"Are you and Max planning to get married?"

"Yes, it's just a matter of time. I've been the one stalling. Some days when Max is busy, when he doesn't give me enough attention, I think, This isn't going to work! But what about you? I heard all about your break-up from Barry." She gave Catherine a sympathetic look.

"Oh, I don't know. Right now that sort of thing seems a long way away."

"What about you and Barry, are you interested in him? He's an awfully nice man, isn't he?"

Catherine looked at Barry standing in the open doorway. He was watching her with a warm yet patronizing smile, and suddenly she remembered one of their dates, at a French restaurant downtown. Between the appetizers and the entrées the waiter had brought them each a glass dish containing a tiny scoop of pale sorbet. Barry immediately put his arm around her, leaned close, and said loudly, "Do you know what that is? It's sorbet. It's to cleanse the palate." She shrugged him off, embarrassed and annoyed at his presumption that she had never been to such a fine restaurant before meeting him, that she would not recognize sorbet served between courses and might do something socially appalling with it.

"He's very nice," Catherine concurred, and she thought of the fact that he had won citizenship awards in school, that that was the sort of person he was.

Later that afternoon music swelled through the house before the dinner party. The kitchen was lit, all the polished surfaces winking at each other. Max was on the phone for a long time, listening to the pitch of a woman on the island who was sick with cancer and wanted him to help pay for her operation. She was not even a friend, only someone who had heard of his wealth. Catherine couldn't imagine such presumption. "Wasn't she embarrassed to ask you?"

"Apparently not," Max said, the corners of his mouth crimping.

He turned to Claire, who was supervising the preparation of the appetizers. "I said yes. You don't think I was being too generous?"

That was Max, to whom generosity was something he needed help to curb.

The guests had yet to arrive. Holly Palmer's "Lickerish Man" filled the room. Max was laughing, pirouetting Claire around the living-room floor. She was wearing white, like a bride—a white blouse and a silky white skirt down to her ankles. The sash around the waistband of her skirt was hung with tiny bells, which tinkled when she moved. He lifted her easily and she kicked her feet in playful protest. Catherine could hardly watch them. She remembered being a child, dancing with her father to a record on the turntable, her tiny bright reflection filling his sight as though she was all that existed in the world. The doors to the deck were open, and as the couple danced the wind blew dry leaves into the house. Later in the evening the sky would lighten with the moon's ascent, and the ocean would glow white like the inside of a crisp apple.

Barry, who was assembling a salad, sent Catherine out to the yard for herbs from the garden. The door of the cabin had been unlatched by the wind and it banged dolefully open and shut, the latch never connecting with the nail. From a distance the house was light and warmth; the pottery Max and Claire collected was sleek on the shelves, its surfaces smooth as flesh. The house was all texture and sensuality, polished maple, slabs of slate, chunky concrete. There were figs on a plate on the kitchen counter, collapsing open at a touch to yield heart-shaped wedges of pink, seedy flesh.

When the dinner guests arrived they ate indoors in the dining room; the candles on the table melted slowly, wax sliding down the silver holders. Catherine admired the diamonds and gold twisted into a wedding ring on one of the women, and Claire turned to Max at the head of the table, teasing, "Where's my ring, Max?"

He stroked her arm, giving her a long, lingering look. It was the gaze of a man in love. Catherine, watching, thought that that was how other men she had been with had looked at her once, and it was this that had caused her to love them back. And when their adoration of her disappeared, her own feelings for them eroded into contempt.

"Well, you haven't asked me to marry you yet," Max murmured.

Claire paused, then retorted, "Fear of rejection!"

An hour later the deck was crowded with party guests, and Max and Claire were busy being hosts. Barry wove through the groups of people, searching for someone he knew. Catherine followed him, marvelling. He had taken her to cocktail parties before where she had watched him in action, looking, as he put it, "For someone *interesting*." He would eventually mutter the recognizable last name of someone in business or the arts or, simply, "society," then grab her hand and pull her with him in that person's direction, his short legs pumping in his eagerness to reach that person before someone else did. Now, in a rush of pleasure, he said, "Oh, good, the Hudsons are here, and look, is that the Williamsons? Delightful. Excellent!" And suddenly she was standing on the edge of a group of people, watching Barry backslap the men and hug their wives, exclaiming over them.

He introduced her, but beyond a perfunctory handshake no one spoke to her. These people were older, conservative, with certain lifestyles and certain friends. As if through the wrong end of a telescope she saw them laughing over their shared jokes—their heads flung back, their mouths gaping, five sets of thirty teeth, some surely false in their perfection, showing. Their laughter was sharp and horrifying, like the barking of vicious dogs. The women wore heavy gold jewellery and clusters of diamonds, pendants like amulets, though their dresses were in the simple style of the island. Their husbands were well-to-do and famous—famous for their wealth, or wealthy because of their fame. They were snug in their accomplishments, the wits at every dinner party. When they glanced at Catherine it was in expectation of her fawning laughter, the way a television comedian might glance at his sidekick. Their shiny eyes looked right through her, as though she was transparent. It made her feel as if she didn't exist.

Eventually she excused herself—Barry was too busily engaged to notice her departure, and the others had never noticed her presence to begin with—and wandered around the deck alone. Men smiled at her from various groups but none invited her in. There were plates of sushi on tables under the eaves, and clusters of half-empty wine bottles. Max was talking to a woman in a long flowered dress and, watching him, Catherine admired his social ease; he was the best-looking man there, built from some superior stock.

After a while Barry noticed her absence and came to her side. He was flushed and happy. "Wonderful party. Such interesting people here. Some of us are going for a tour of the garden, are you coming?"

She followed him. The garden was vast. It went on and on, a maze of phlox, roses, larkspur, paintbrush. Then the vegetable patch, and kiwi vines snaking along trellises, hung with hard furred fruit. It was not a garden, it was acreage. In their group there was a retired politician, an internationally famous sculptor, Queen's Counsel lawyers, no one less. One of them, a doctor who seemed a little drunk, his wine glass clutched in an unsteady hand, fell into step beside her and said, inexplicably, "You seem to the manor born."

Catherine looked down at herself, thinking of her rusty Volvo, her rented studio apartment, and said, "Why would you say that? I don't even know any of these people."

She stopped and turned, looking back at the house through the thickly leafed branches of the plum trees. On the deck people were drinking, their mouths opening and closing in conversation and laughter. What were they saying to each other? What did these people have to talk about? It was dark now, and the huge sky above was a black bowl full of chipped stars. The flames of the citronella candles twisted and smoked. She glimpsed Claire's figure inside the house, through a picture window, and Max beside her. Now Claire turned, laughing at something someone said, and moved out of the windowframe. There was just Max. Watching him, Catherine was struck by the poignancy of the space between them. How many men had she desired from a distance? It had been that way with Peter. Yet once their relationship was actualized, she had grown to hate him. It seemed there was a brief time of bliss, then, all too soon, you were looking at this person, the one you had once admired, with rage. She remembered coming home one day and finding Peter slumped again in front of his camera equipment, his longish hair unwashed, his thin shoulders bent forward in concentration. He had not even acknowledged her presence, and such hatred rose up in her that her mouth filled with acid. It seemed impossible that once she had looked at him the way she now looked at Max, that perhaps they weren't even so different. It was only that she had gotten to know Peter, whereas Max was still pristine, perfect in his mystery.

After their walk they gathered in the living room by the lit fireplace. There was supposed to be dancing, but the wine had made everyone sleepy, and already it was near midnight. Barry complimented Claire on her blouse, and Max said, "Why don't you show us the other outfit I bought you, sweetheart."

"Which one?"

"The one I like. You know. The outfit we bought when we told the sales clerk you were my daughter." He nudged her off the arm of the sofa where they were sitting. There was a chorus from the guests: "Yes, Claire, let's have a fashion show!" They were sitting in groups around the fireplace, Barry with his feet up on the ottoman, the women on the stone bench with their backs to the fire, their men on the floor with their long legs stretched out.

"No, I can't do that," Claire contested.

"Yes you can, baby. Go on, do it for me."

Claire demurred, but eventually went upstairs to change. Max stared across the coffee table at Catherine. "A fantasy, see. I told Claire about it."

Catherine shook her head, as if what she had heard was a hallucination. It was too hot in the room, from the fire and the crowded bodies, and her eyes burned.

Barry watched Max silently. The other guests laughed and someone started to say, teasingly, "Max, you dirty-minded . . ." but trailed off.

The guests shifted awkwardly in their seats; there was a crackle of tension as well as anticipation in the air. Catherine thought that Max looked different to her now, another person really. Maybe all you have to do is stay with someone long enough, and you learn everything you need to know about them.

Claire came down the curving staircase, entering the room slowly. She wore a green-and-blue tartan skirt pierced with a huge safety pin, and dark green socks up to her bare knees, which were scuffed as though she really were a child who had been playing in the schoolyard. She was so small and thin, her body so delicately structured, that even the narrow starched shirt was too large for her, the cuffs too long. Her eyes were solemn, a bit anxious. She stood in front of the upturned faces of the group, her palms flat against the sides of her thighs.

"Aahh!" Max was delighted. His pupils dilated with pleasure at the sight of her, properly costumed. He held his arms out and she ran to his embrace. "Look at you!" he murmured, stroking her arm, her hair, admiring her as though she were a child whose very existence was cause for exclamation. Claire glanced up at him and began rolling up the waistband of her skirt to shorten it, and neither of them noticed the too-loud laughter from their guests, or the way they were being watched, as though they were being seen for the first time.

Later that night Barry walked Catherine to the cabin and then did not leave her room. They lay on the bed under the drape of mosquito netting, his arms around her and her head on his shoulder. She was very sleepy and her head throbbed, a band of pain stretching from temple to temple. She longed to go to sleep like this. The thin fabric of the net stirred as they shifted their bodies. She had left the bathroom light on and the door open all evening, forgetting, and the room was filled with mosquitoes. Barry turned her face to his and kissed her, and she allowed herself to be kissed. It mattered so little. When was the last time she had responded to anything? It seemed a long time ago. Catherine ran her fingers through Barry's grey hair and settled back on his shoulder. His breath was warm against her skin and smelled like apple juice. The bulk of him was comforting, and she recalled her own father with an ache—the way when she was a child he would sit by her bedside and read to her while she fought sleep, clinging to consciousness so she could savour those fleeting moments of their intimacy, his large veined hand on her shoulder, his deep voice reading on. It was all she had wanted out of love. But then she grew up, and he averted his eyes from her tall, budding female form when he kissed her hastily goodnight in the hall outside her bedroom.

Barry reached over to touch her breast and she deftly, drowsily shrugged him off. She felt herself drifting towards sleep. The last thing she saw was the shed snakeskin—an intact grey ribbon, crinkly as crinoline—that she had picked up on her walk earlier that day, cradling it in both her hands. Tomorrow she would leave this island. Outside, Max's land was dark, and the moon, caught behind a skein of cloud, no longer illuminated anything.

A FAITHFUL HUSBAND

ITALY WAS PART of her dream. "You should not have to be thirty before you see Rome," Melody's high school art teacher had once told the class, and she had never forgotten. For her twenty-ninth birthday her husband Gordon surprised her with a plane ticket and a hotel voucher. "Honey, go have a good time," he said with a brave smile when she protested that she didn't want to go without him. "I'd be useless there, I'm afraid. Besides, I'm not interested in a bunch of churches and old buildings." He stroked her cheek and turned back to the afternoon movie on television.

That first day in Rome, from the back of a skidding taxi, Melody looked at the city through her husband's eyes. It was as though everything before her was shrouded in grey, in the fog of depression. She realized that his lack of awe had gradually become hers too; she had slowed down, seized up, closed herself in order to be with Gordon, who was sixty-five years old. Rome was crowded streets, pollution, narrow hawk-faced women patrolling the sidewalks in tight black clothes. It was a bad exchange rate and statues whose copies were more impressive than the crumbling, verdigris originals could be. She looked at Rome this way and saw that yes, this was a way of looking at the world—as a collection of bad smells in the nose, a world of bother and inconvenience, crowded by people who got in the way.

She knew instinctively what Gordon would think of her small, exquisite hotel room with its wrought-iron balcony overlooking a courtyard filled with flowers. The television broadcasted Italian channels, and those only intermittently. There was no room service, and the restaurant next door did not open until past eight. At home he demanded his dinner early, before six if possible, and she knew that the heavy doses of olive oil in the local diet would upset his digestion. She could see him cursing and complaining about every aspect of this experience; she could see him trodding through the ruins of civilization, dismissing centuries with a shrug.

Over the next few days she went everywhere with her camera and her sketchpad. She walked through the brown ruin of the Colosseum, and took a tour bus past the verdant valley which had once held the Circus Maximus and was now strewn with joggers. At the Trevi Fountain she tossed a five-hundred-lira coin over her shoulder, along with the other tourists from all over Europe and Japan. In the Church of St. Peter in Chains she stood in front of a statue of Moses by Michelangelo and stared at it until its blank marble eyes glowed and threatened to rise and smite her. Her husband's voice played like a tape in the back of her mind: "Nothing but churches and old buildings . . . Hey, *I* could have painted that . . . I wish we could find a Wendy's or an IHOP . . ." But then she was on the Palatine Hill overlooking the ruins of the Roman Forum, the crumbling columns white as bone, something swept away his voice until she was herself again. She wanted to shed him like a heavy sweater on a day that had started cloudy and become clear.

And then she met Stephen. A mutual friend had given her his number before she left for Italy; he was a travel writer from Canada who was living in Rome for a few months, writing articles about Italy for magazines and newspapers back home. They met for coffee one afternoon and Melody was immediately drawn to his lopsided smile. He was young; his eyes were a dark green that made her think of deep pools of water. He was not especially handsome but that made his charm all the more extraordinary. While they talked he tapped his foot on the floor, bit his fingernails, threw back his head and laughed. He had so much energy he seemed unable to stay contained inside his body.

They saw each other often during the days that followed. Stephen chain-smoked, shared green bottles of wine with her over lunch, took her to the Vatican and, pointing ahead, said, "There is eternity." The wind swept through the courtyard and clouds flew across the blue fresco sky. As they walked around the Piazza san Pietro, Melody pressed closer to him so she could smell his skin, his exposed neck. She breathed and breathed. The wind was cold and tasted like melon on her tongue. And all she could think of was sex. There were only so many days they were accorded together and with each passing hour it was becoming a necessity that she feel his mouth smiling upon hers. But she had only known husbands to philander; she had been secretly shocked when her girlfriends had confessed their own indiscretions to her over drinks or a restaurant meal. One-night stands with men they met at business conventions, or standing in line at the post office or the supermarket. This was a man's territory, and for it to be a woman's also felt frightening to her, destabilizing. Now there was Stephen, and already she felt a star of jealousy bursting in her chest when she caught his eyes sliding to the exposed thighs of a pretty woman wearing a miniskirt, or when he met an acquaintance on the street and exchanged what to her seemed unnecessarily intimate kisses, the Italian way, firm and lingering on both cheeks. He was smelling another's skin, taken in, inhaled by another. Melody wanted to own him, to have all his senses focused on her.

"Have you ever been in love?"

"Oh, sure," he said with a smile. "But I never let anyone get too close. I'm just not the settling-down type. I mean, who knows where I'll be in a year?"

She thought of how Gordon liked to touch her young, taut skin, and how she sometimes liked to pull at his, the ruined surfaces of his face, the rings of Venus around his neck, laughing at how his flesh stayed pinched and raised where she tugged it, whereas her own sprang back. Now she craved Stephen's impatient male energy, his smooth hands with their bitten nails hungrily exploring her body. She had never felt with her husband what she could only guess was the passion she was feeling towards Stephen.

Together they walked through Rome, and she did not enter any of the shops because there was nothing she wanted to purchase, nothing she wanted to keep but what flared in the air between them. In the back seat of a taxi she rubbed her hands together and said, "I'm cold"—struggling to keep the child out of her voice—"feel them," and placed her hands over his. He glanced at her in mute surprise and then stroked her fingers nervously while he continued to converse in halting Italian with the gesticulating driver.

"I find you reassuring," she ventured.

He did not look at her. "Why? I'm not, you know."

In the Piazza di Spagna they sat on the bottom step in silence. When two girls came up to them asking for cigarettes he extended his pack and Melody wished then that she, too, smoked. She had to restrain herself from leaning over and kissing the edge of his smile.

And then, late one night, he took her to a nightclub on one of the side streets near her hotel. Stephen grasped her hand and pulled her through the pulsating darkness, the press of bodies, the beautiful Italian men and women with their dark eyes and flashing teeth, onto the dance floor. Everything felt hot and close—the thick, dusty air, the smell of sweat and perfume and alcohol, the strangers bumping up against her. Melody was wearing a white halter dress, and the black light in the club lit her up so she glowed. Stephen smiled at her, shouted something, but the music was thunderous, pounding up from the floorboards, rolling over them in waves from the walls. She tried to shout back, but when he threw his hands up and shook his head, they simply gave themselves over to the music and danced. Gordon was now far away; his scornful voice gone and in its place, finally, was life waiting.

"Did you like the club?" Stephen asked as they walked back to her hotel.

"It was amazing," she said, and was immediately struck by such longing that she couldn't continue. Perhaps sensing what she felt, he reached out and took her hand, squeezing it in his.

In the hotel he followed her into the old-fashioned elevator suspended on two cables behind a wrought-iron door and twin inner doors with panels of frosted glass. They rose past the other floors which were visible to them through the glass. Then the elevator stopped, or was stuck rather, on the third floor, and they had to climb the remaining flights of stairs to her room.

He walked into the room behind her and she unlatched the tall doors to the balcony. They stepped out into the warm night air.

"Oh, but this is fine. Fine," he said, next to her, and she could trace the shape of his mouth forming the words. He raised his arm and pointed at a blurry streak in the sky. "There's the Milky Way."

It was a smudge, with a few etiolated stars. She looked at it in silence, hardly seeing it, conscious only of his presence next to her.

Stephen turned back into the room, then stood there looking at her. She was aware that his life was so unlike hers, that he had made choices entirely different from the ones she had made. His future was full of possibilities that were closed to her because of Gordon. Next to them, the narrow, single bed swelled to fill the room.

"Goodnight," she said, moving into his embrace, his mouth that opened on hers.

And her husband was a thought, a fish, that swam rapidly to the surface. Melody pushed it back down and it sunk, the fish curled up and sunk to the bottom of the ocean. It seemed foolish that she had thought this would feel wrong when it felt as if it were the one true thing. It was like being only dimly aware of being hungry or thirsty until the full plate or glass was set in front of you, and the force of your appetite overwhelmed you. When they drew apart his eyes were squinted against the light from the bedside table, possibly against the too-close vision of her. She slid her fingers through his hair, the thick layers of glossy brown so different from Gordon's crimpy white hair, thin as floss.

They lay down awkwardly on the narrow bed and he kept his arms around her the entire time, which seemed a gesture of uncalled-for tenderness. The fish stirred at the bottom of the ocean; wave after wave, a thousand leagues, closed over it. His penis lay, huge, against her hip. She wanted him inside her and then he was. It was as she imagined it would be. All that she had with Gordon, the conversations and emotional negotiations, what they had both risked and forsaken for each other, was of no consequence. Her husband was, in the moment Stephen entered her, displaced forever.

He did not stay. The next morning he arrived early at her hotel. The lobby was set behind the reception desk so that, from her seat on one of the floral sofas, she could watch the people coming and going through the front doors where the hotel name was written in gold script. It was a fine day, and the sun glinted off the shiny surfaces. Melody saw him enter the hotel and stand at the front desk talking to the proprietor, a middle-aged midget who, when he wasn't handling guests, spent his time in the dining room, watching football and tippling from a bottle of brandy.

Stephen saw her reflection approaching him in a mirror

before he saw Melody, and in a moment of confusion he turned to the reflection instead of to her. He touched her lightly on the arm and they walked out into the warm day.

Neither said anything about what had happened the night before. They walked in silence down the cobbled streets, past crumbling buildings with stone façades. It was finally hot, and Melody felt perspiration gathering in the hollows of her body under her black sweater. She tried to think of something to say and couldn't. She could talk about her husband, whom Stephen had immediately dubbed "the old man," but she had noticed how he seemed to discourage this. If she mentioned Gordon he would give a shrug and say nothing. Now it seemed they were only enduring each other's company. In the sticky sunlight, she could not imagine ever having sought his hand because hers was cold.

They walked through a park where the leaves were golden and persimmon trees dropped their overripe red fruit on the ground around them. They passed young couples intently twined together on the grass, and busts of famous Romans on pedestals, some wearing a vandal's painted moustache and lolling tongue, some noseless or decapitated.

They came out on the other side of the park onto the Piazza di Spagna, on the landing overlooking the steps, with the Church of Triniti Dei Monti behind them. Tourists were stumbling, laughing, into the fountain to drink from its waters, holding out uncapped Evian bottles. It had come to be a tradition, like throwing a coin into the Trevi so they would return to Rome someday. The warmth of the day lay over everything.

Stephen started down the stairs, and as she followed him, trying not to tread on the hands and feet of the people on the steps who were writing or drawing, she said, "Right now, somebody's standing at the top of the stairs, above us, looking down at us and thinking, 'Who are those people? What is their story?'"

He laughed gently. "'How did they meet? Are they related?'"

"'And are they happy?'" What would she have said if someone had asked her that? If someone looked directly into her eyes and asked, "Are you in love?" Even a day ago she would have said yes. Of course. She loved her husband, it was what she had to believe for the marriage to continue. Now she would see Stephen's face in the lamplight, feel the corner of his mouth beneath her fingertips, and wonder how this could sit alongside a love of Gordon, from whom she had already retreated so far that when she tried to miss him, she could not. Already she could imagine exchanging him for Stephen, she could imagine never seeing again the man she had married.

"Ah, soon you'll be home." Stephen looked down at her, but she could not tell what he was thinking. "Among your friends, in your apartment." He did not say, With your husband.

"I'm sad," she confessed. She said it again in the taxi he called to take them to the airport. The driver was young and impossibly handsome as some Italian men were, and she saw the flash of his eyes regarding her in the rearview mirror, his long, dense lashes. As he drove he unrolled the passenger window and chatted with another man driving a gelato truck alongside them. They stopped together at intersections and continued their conversation as if uninterrupted. "I'm sad," she said as Rome fled past the window—motorcycles, black-dressed women, Versace and Bulgari, cafés and dead popes, the unimaginable ruins.

"Why are you sad?" he said patiently. "Don't be. Your life is elsewhere, Melody."

The night before she had whispered, "Please stay," and Stephen had shaken his head and said, "No. It'll be harder if I stay." She had never pleaded for anyone before, but he could not have known that. He had sat on the end of the narrow bed, looking down at himself disconsolately, and said, "Why? I don't understand." And she was helpless, without the words to explain, except to say, "I want you to stay," and when she asked for a reason as to why he would not, he replied, "I can't explain."

"Try."

He was silent for a while, staring down at his hands in his lap. Then he said simply, resolutely, "I don't want you close to me. And I don't want to be close to you."

She drew in her breath so sharply it stung her. She thought of her husband's warm, wiry embrace, his fervent words, "I can't get you close enough!" Once there had been a time when it delighted her, when it did not suffocate her.

At the airport, among the crowds, they stood and kissed. Behind her closed eyes Melody heard dimly the creak of luggage wheels along the waxy floor, the blurred voices speaking foreign languages, the shriek of the metal detector. Stephen took her upper arms in his hands as though he was bracing her and said, "You have no reason to be sad."

So she forced a smile and, looking into his green eyes, tried out the first of the many lies she would start to tell. "No. All right, I'm not sad."

"I will miss you," he said quietly. "But maybe it's always like this. A few days with another person, and you're used to them. Anyone."

She could have been anyone.

Melody had married Gordon five years ago, but what started off as one thing had already become another. She was discovering that to have someone share his life with her was not the thing she thought she had always desired. Gordon was divorced, with the knobby knees and outthrust shoulder blades of an old man. Upon retirement he gave up his conservative suits and began wearing clothes from another era, jackets of imitation suede that felt like the surface of a pool table, and shoes that split at the sides over his bunions. On his list of things he never wanted to do again, number one was "dance." Most nights they were in bed before ten, lying side by side and holding hands; he fell instantly, passionately asleep, as if sleep were a lover he was hurrying to embrace, while she lay awake looking at the pebbled ceiling of their bedroom, flexing her feet in boredom. A few blocks away from their downtown condominium, the night-clubs were not even beginning to fill.

She had become afraid that his every movement, his every word, was working like a chamois cloth to blur and finally erase her love for him. He was constantly calibrating the rhythm and timbre of his heartbeat; the state of his bowels obsessed him. Every white spot on his thin, hairy forearms was skin cancer, every forgotten name at a cocktail party he insisted on leaving early was the first sign of Alzheimer's. Yet the marriage was a mistake she had been eager to make. In part, it was a final flout-ing of her critical family and her concerned friends, an act of rebellion. She had displayed him on her arm as a man displays a beautiful woman. Together they commanded the attention she craved, and if there was not envy in the second glances, well, no one knew of their private life together. No one had witnessed how he left his wife for her, or the ridicule he had swallowed from his children. And, at first, his physical weak-nesses only roused protective impulses in Melody. As a child she'd taken home stray animals, always shared her handful of jelly beans with her classmates. Her relationship with Gordon seemed only an extension of these things.

Also, he had made promises to her. "I'll always be here," he said, "for better or for worse." It puzzled her that when he said this now, in bed in the greying light of late evening, his jowly face crumpled against the pillow, his arm locked around her like a length of chain, it could sound so different. Like a threat.

Their relationship had been an education at first and then it seemed to become something that hindered her learning. She began to feel that life was elsewhere. At night she dreamed he was again placing the ring on her finger and she was longing to cry out "No," but the church was filled with his colleagues from the law firm and she knew she could not embarrass him in front of them. Then the ring changed, metamorphosed on her finger into a washer, a small rubber band, a Cartier rolling ring whose interlocking bands broke apart and rolled onto the floor. When he saw this he pulled out a pair of handcuffs and clamped them on her wrists, bending to kiss her under the priest's approving gaze. She was not subtle in her dreams and she awoke from them in a panic.

Sometimes she caught herself staring blankly at Gordon as he watched television in the middle of the afternoon, the tinny dialogue of the soap operas distracting her from her drawings, wondering when and how he would die. Cancer, a heart attack, a stroke? Would it be sudden or protracted? A series of strokes had left his mother in an old age home flanked by angels of caritas and a dingy lawn, all seventy pounds of her slumped over in a wheelchair. Gordon had taken her to meet his mother before they were married, and this had felt as much like an offer of commitment as when he had actually proposed. His mother was sitting at a table in the recreation room with half a dozen other women frozen into position like corpses, hands like claws raised in mid-air, mouths open in toothless snarls. She was a soft, bird-like remnant of a person with blind brown eyes that had seen nothing for the past decade. She wore a pale pink sweatshirt embroidered with a daisy, its size and style something an eight-year-old might wear. Melody became aware of the stylish leather trenchcoat she herself was wearing, and the incongruity of her black heels on the floor that was marbled with urine.

Gordon knelt in front of the old woman. She was so tiny that his head and shoulders blocked her out. "Hi, Mom, it's Gordon," he said in a gentle, cajoling voice. "Remember me?"

Melody could feel the tension in his body, the misgiving. His mother had not recognized him in years. She held her breath, her heart twisting with pity.

"Mom?"

One of the old ladies' bowels loosened, and the ripe smell clouded the air. Melody glanced at the faces around the table but none of them were present enough to even look shamed.

"Of course. You were my baby," his mother said suddenly, in a voice too big for her diminished body. It was a schoolteacher's voice, strident, demanding, the single strand of strength left in her. "Oh, you were so small, Gordy, I was afraid I'd hurt you. You were so tiny, there in my arms. I didn't know how to take care of you."

"Well, you did a wonderful job, Mom," Gordon said. He stroked the cotton sleeve of her sweatshirt; the cuff slid over her knuckles. "I love you very much."

"It was so cold in the winters, and there you were, so tiny, oh, you were such a tiny thing . . ."

"I'm big now," he said, laughing gently. "You were a great mom."

Melody scuffed her heels against the slick floor. At that moment she was certain he loved her also. She had not believed it entirely until now, until she heard him saying it to his mother in the same voice he had said it to her. She looked at the drooling, nodding old woman and could not see in her face any glimmer of the person she had been at twenty-five, yet Gordon had once shown her a photograph of his mother as a young woman, wearing a dress covered in what looked like antique lace, but then must have been just lace. His mother had classic, ageless features and translucent skin. Her eyes were shining and spaced wide apart.

Melody tried to imagine Gordon as a helpless infant and for a moment she imagined he was being passed on to her not as an old man but as that baby. Now it was up to her not to hurt him, not to drop him. She looked down at her black shoes in silence. What do I know, she thought—what little do I know.

"Mom? There's someone I'd like you to meet." Gordon turned and smiled at Melody, reaching for her hand, until he was holding the hands of both women. "This is Melody."

"Um, hi," Melody said awkwardly, in a voice she hoped conveyed warmth and sincerity.

His mother rubbed her frail wrists together and gazed straight through Melody with watery eyes framed by a few sparse lashes. "You were so tiny," she announced. "Such a tiny thing. I didn't know how to help you."

"Um, Mrs. Carstairs, I'm Melody."

"So tiny . . ."

Gordon mercifully interrupted. "Mom, do you know how old you are? You're ninety-one! You turned ninety-one last week!"

The old woman swivelled her head in the direction of his voice and exclaimed, "Oh, my! Really?"

Melody felt relieved, at least until his mother added, "Lord, I want to die."

Not long after that, Gordon introduced her to his youngest daughter, who was still six years older than she was. At that time Janice was the only one of his children who was still on speaking terms with Gordon after hearing about his relationship with Melody. They went for breakfast one blustery morning in a hotel dining room with patterned pastel furniture and brass rails. His daughter was waiting for them when they arrived, and when she rose to greet them Melody saw the other woman give her a swift look of surprise, as though she had expected her to be different, a gold digger with visible claws. Melody had deliberately worn a turtleneck and no make-up that morning. His daughter was more beautiful than she expected; she had hair down to her waist and her father's dark eyes.

Over a breakfast of eggs hollandaise—Melody, who was not naturally thin like Gordon and his daughter, ordered a poached egg and dry wheat toast, and when it arrived Janice looked at it and said wryly, "That looks like a breakfast Grandma would have!"—the three of them seemed to form the points of a triangle, each opposed to the others. As Melody ate her breakfast, her left eyelid started to twitch, something it did only under profound stress, and she had to place her forefinger over it. Despite this, Janice seemed to like her, and when they said goodbye, Gordon hugging her tightly while Melody stood aside, she smiled and said, "Will I get a half-brother or -sister? You two would have beautiful children!"

The matter of children was, well, another matter. Their lovemaking was circumscribed, mostly a matter of tongues and fingers, joined hands in the middle of the night, nothing else. When their affair began, in downtown hotels in mid-afternoon, sometimes in his office with its voracious views of the harbour and its portraits on the wall of the law firm's founders, it had involved nothing but oral sex. She had thought it was because he was married and felt guilty about doing more, but as it turned out he couldn't do more. When he lay on top of her he was soft as a woman and sometimes, curiously, in her dreams he did indeed take a woman's shape, with long curls and an ambiguous, shifting visage. He touched her so gently it made her ache. At first this was enough and then—anyone could have told her, but she wouldn't have believed—it was not. After they were married she developed a hunger she tried to ignore. Surely it was a man's place to be hungry, in that way. But Gordon was not, though sometimes he tried to be; sometimes he nudged her awake in the middle of the night to climb on top of her, panting hopefully into the pillow next to her ear. His shoulder blades fitted into her palms, but his brief, weak erection would subside as soon as he entered her, and then there was only the bleakness of the bluish light in the room, the sound of a car swishing past on the street outside, the pulsing movement of his empty hips, his whispered apology which agonized her. He was old. His insides gurgled with distress as he slid off her, leaving her awake, clenched in the shame that had somehow transferred itself from him to her, staining her.

She wondered what the girls in the nightclub down the street would think if they could look through the window of their bedroom and see her lying next to him as he crunched a disk of cherry-flavoured Maalox, his fingers tenderly probing the region of his stomach, seeking out the source of pains both phantom and real.

Gordon embraced retirement, and wanted nothing to do with his former life. The competitive nature and sharp intellect she had admired when she worked for him had somehow vanished.

He liked to spend his days reading newspapers, lingering over the crossword and the daily Scrabble clues. He watched television shows that appealed to people of her generation. In this way he was not old—he surprised her constantly with his knowledge of popular culture—but in other ways he had given up. In his journal he wrote not personal thoughts or feelings but the titles and plots of matinees he had seen that day, so that he might remember the entertainments of his life if not its more meaningful moments. There were very few interesting things in the world, he maintained. He had never travelled outside of North America and had no interest in going anywhere where he might be deprived of movie theatres and American-style hotel rooms, where he might suffer from traveller's diarrhea and the straits of strangers.

Perhaps the stress of their courtship had worn him out. He had been so afraid she would leave him if they got married that he had made her promise, again and again, that she meant to stay. "I promise I won't leave you," Melody had written in a letter one day, and imagined him lying awake next to his wife that night, her letter tucked in among the legal briefs he'd brought to bed, tracing her handwriting with his forefinger and nodding to himself. All right, he would risk everything and believe her. She could see him gravely gathering himself up to leave the security of what he knew—a wife who loved him, looked after him, made sure he ate his vegetables—to become a cliché.

In turn, Gordon promised her he would give her all the time and space she needed to pursue her dream of becoming an artist, but his need for attention made his promise impossible. If she snuck into the sunroom she used as an office to sit at her drafting table with its sketchpads and charcoals, she would within minutes hear him moving disconsolately around the apartment, sighing grandly, picking up and then putting down the remote control, flipping the pages of a magazine, opening and closing the refrigerator door. She could feel his eyes on her back through the French doors. Her concentration would splinter, break, and she would leave her desk to accompany him to the restaurant meal, the walk around the neighbourhood, the matinee, hoping this was enough—his glad smile, his hand tucking hers into the warm burrow of his jacket pocket, his adoring eyes. Hoping that marriage could be a replacement for art, that it, too, could be a life's work.

"But I don't understand. I was happy," Gordon was saying. They were lying in bed the night after her return from Rome and Melody was curled away from him, her muffled voice saying that she thought the marriage wasn't working, that maybe they had made a mistake. But only a week ago she had woken, her hair tangled in the sunlight through the blinds, and reached for him, her arms wrapping around his neck like a child's, her cotton nightshirt soft and slipping in his hands. Now she was hunched into herself like a sick creature. "Is there something you're not telling me?"

And she learned something new about herself when she said, "Of course not."

"All right then, all right," he said quickly, struggling to compose himself. He tried to turn her face towards his and, when she wouldn't accommodate him, he rolled her onto her back and lay on top of her. She was floppy as a doll. The bottom of her nightshirt was pulled up to her stomach and she felt him naked against her thigh. He was soft and tiny. She could never feel him even when he was inside her. "But I thought we made a long-term commitment to each other. I love you!"

Melody flinched. It was dark in the room and she could hardly see him. It was after ten o'clock, he should be asleep. He needed his sleep. She didn't love him. And if love could disappear so suddenly, was it ever there at all?

"Are you saying you want us to get a divorce? Jesus! I can't believe this!"

She could say, Yes. As she had once said, "I do." It would liberate her. She saw Stephen's smile flickering behind her eyelids, felt the smoothness of his cheek under her fingers. He had given her a quizzical look when she kept touching his skin. "I just shaved today," he explained, but it was youth that made his skin remarkable. She breathed quietly, her husband's frail weight on top of her. Gordon had been kind to her. He had made sacrifices on behalf of her. How he had suffered when one of his daughters would not speak to him for months other than to call him an old fool. How Melody had woken up in the morning to find him looking at her sadly, touching a ringlet of her hair, thinking of his scornful daughter. And still he had chosen her.

"Is that what you want?" His voice was incredulous.

He had only to keep asking for her to say yes, but then he fell silent. Above her, he kept shaking his head, as though to try to shake something out of it. She knew because she had loved men before whom she had tried to shake out of her head and could not. Pity welled in her. Melody thought of Stephen, the hotel room in Rome. His smile, his eyes. Please, she tried to communicate to him. Don't go.

"I can't believe this! After everything! After . . ." Gordon climbed off her, lay down next to her, covered his eyes. She breathed a small sigh of relief, pressed her legs together. He swallowed, several times. "After I put up with what everyone said. My daughter. Friends telling me I was being ridiculous. Your juvenile drawings . . ."

He stopped. The room was silent but for the sound of his rapid swallowing. Anger rose in her, then subsided into mere sadness. She put her hand to the side of his face, a nurse's professional gesture of tenderness, and felt hot moisture. He was crying. He had only cried once before in his life, at his mother's funeral. Yet she was surprised at how little moved she was. And at the duty she nonetheless felt, filial duty, no less than that.

"Everything will be all right," she suggested.

"It'll only be all right if we're together."

It was like a door being shut and locked upon her. Melody whispered, "I won't leave you, then."

"That's good, that's good," the old man muttered. He rubbed her breast through her nightshirt, turned her face towards his and kissed her. She was not only without desire, she was repulsed. The mucousy slip of his tongue in her mouth, the oils on his forehead, his ruined and sagging face. He smelled off to her, a combination of sour musk and something vaguely fecal. He put his hand on the back of her neck and nudged her until she lay between his thighs, his penis in her mouth. With each jolt of his orgasm her spirit crumpled. She gagged as she swallowed, realizing that already she could not clearly picture Stephen's smile, she could no longer smell his skin, only the rank smell of her husband.

SUBURBIA

BELINDA WAS FIRST to arrive at the quay where the bus route terminated. She was wearing a slip dress and platform shoes, and her dark hair was tied back in a ponytail. It was a warm Sunday in early fall; the bus was packed with adolescent girls gone shopping for CDs, make-up or clothes. She emerged with them into the circular station with its shops and restaurants, expecting Jeremy to be waiting for her, carrying bags of groceries for their dinner together. She would immediately be able to pick out his face in the crowd, not because it was the face of a loved one, a father or a husband, but because he would be looking at her helplessly, his head tilted to one side with the burden of his desire for her.

Looking around uncertainly, she shifted the bottle of wine she brought for dinner from one arm to the other. But he was not there. Nearby was a bench by a cul-de-sac where people coming to pick up bus passengers could temporarily park. After she sat down she crossed her legs, uncrossed them, sighed impatiently to mask the pulse of anxiety that had begun its beat inside her chest. That he had not shown up earlier than she had unsettled her. Cars turned and stopped in front of her, passenger doors opened, and she looked inside each one to see if Jeremy was driving. She didn't know what car he'd be in, his own or his wife's; they all looked the same to her anyway, family vans and station wagons painted in muted colours, with middle-aged men at the wheel. She put on her sunglasses and watched the teenagers crossing the quay to the waiting coaches. Many of the girls were beautiful, with clear complexions and the long-limbed, firm-fleshed ease of youth. They were all someone's daughter, someone's student; some of them might even be Jeremy's psychology students, Belinda realized. She knew he eyed his female students wistfully. He claimed to have crushes on one or two of them each semester, and that this was harmless. "They're lovely girls, but it's nothing," he told her. "It's just their youth, the architecture of their bodies, the way they look at me sometimes as if I know the answer to everything." She was reminded of Maslow's theory, that people grow tall and straight and beautiful in the right environments. Were these adolescents beautiful because they were loved? It seemed so, the way their fathers waited patiently for them on this bright, fading day, a slight briskness to the air signifying the end of summer. The way the men called out, "Hello, sweetheart," in their deep, resonant voices, their eyes alight. The girls tossed their backpacks and shopping bags carelessly into the back seat, their bare tanned legs scissoring into the car, their brushed hair floating behind them.

Earlier that summer Jeremy had taken her for lunch on the patio of the Thai seafood restaurant at the quay, and over the garlic prawns and saffron rice he'd said plaintively, "I've always been in love with you."

It was a hot day, the height of summer, sun beating down on the umbrella above their table. Belinda watched twin lines of perspiration run down his temples from under his sparse silver hair. "More than your family?" she asked, keeping her voice light. "If you had to make a choice, in a flood or an earthquake, and you could only save them, or me, which would it be?"

He looked at her in consternation. "How can you ask that?"

Although she had only been teasing, Belinda felt as if he had already abandoned her.

"Genetic imperative states it," he continued, in his professorial tone. "I would virtually have no choice in that moment but to ensure the survival of my own DNA."

And now, just when Belinda thought he might not show, Jeremy came striding towards her from the direction of the market. He wore a Tilley hat jammed down on his head and a beige silk shirt and pants with creases in them. He was smiling feverishly, all his features stretched sideways by the pull of his smile.

It took a while for him to reach her even with his long legs, time for her to observe him in the detached, slightly contemptuous way she reserved for him now. It seemed a long time ago that she had sat in class listening to him, wanting him. The dry white lines across his forehead, the creases at his ears, only made him more attractive to her. It was the distance between them, his unattainability, that sparked her infatuation. When he turned his sharp, intellectual gaze upon her she was silenced. Sometimes, before a class, she would pace in front of his office door, her heart pounding, wondering if he was inside. His office, with its antique lamps and red Persian rugs, was lush compared to the institutional poverty of the academic building with its failing computers and scratched desks, its linoleum floors and torn posters tacked to corkboards lining the halls. The university, despite its green grounds and gracious maples, its golf course and garden, was nonetheless so pinched for funds that the administration had ordered the water fountains in all the buildings removed rather than replace the rusty pipes. When Belinda walked past Jeremy in the halls he would say, a little mockingly, "Hello, Miss Belinda, how are you?" and her breath would catch in her throat because he seemed not of the world of noisy, rushing students in their jeans and baggy nylon coats, carrying the burden of their books, but beyond.

"My God, have you been waiting here all this time?" Now he reached her breathlessly, embraced her. She resisted him at first, upset with him for letting her feel forgotten, but his arms were strong and he held her tightly as if to squeeze the life out of her. "I parked the car, and when the buses came in and I didn't see you, I went into the market to do some shopping."

"I've been here for the past twenty minutes," Belinda said rather sullenly.

"I must have missed you. How could I have missed you? Oh, it's so good to see you. I was watching for you, I was looking for your face . . ."

They began walking towards his car. He kept turning to look down at her with an expression of helpless delight. When he stopped to kiss her, impulsively, his lips felt dry against hers and she pulled away, giggling to hide her discomfort. The sunlight was harsh and flat on his face, emphasizing the wrinkles fanning from his eyes, the pouches of sagging flesh, the white spots of solar damage. He took her hand in his, squeezing it, and she was conscious that they must look to others like father and daughter, united after a long absence.

Jeremy parked the Toyota in the garage and for a moment they just sat there. For the first time he was going to make dinner for her, in his house. His wife Deirdre was away for the weekend, visiting their son who was attending college out of town. Belinda was aware of her own breathing. Jeremy pulled the car keys out of the ignition and expelled what sounded like a held breath. "Well. Here we are."

She looked around her for something to say. The air in the garage smelled of damp wood and shovels. Above them two dusty red canoes were mounted on the ceiling, sleek in their shapes as fish, and she commented on them. They reminded her that Jeremy had always had another life quite different from the one he showed his students, and that it was her curiosity about this other life that had fuelled her interest at first. Belinda could not now imagine him shooting the rapids and suspected neither he nor his wife could see their past selves either, the days when they went swimming with their tow-headed children, when Jeremy was a young academic and dedicated his first textbook "To Deirdre, my beloved wife."

"Well, come in. Mind the dog. You remember Toblerone. Hey, Toby." The chocolate-coloured Labrador came bounding down the hall out of the kitchen, his curved nails clacking on the hardwood floor. Jeremy continued ahead and Belinda was left to fend for herself against the family dog, who sniffed her crotch and unfurled a lascivious tongue.

She had first visited this house two years ago, when Jeremy had a Christmas party here for his class. His wife and son had gone to visit Deirdre's mother, so she hadn't met them, but his daughter was there. They were the same age then, twenty-three. Lisette's beauty was something Jeremy commented on with pride. She was tall and slender, with yellow curls and hard, blazing eyes. Her black minidress was moulded to her body and Belinda could see her walking down the quiet suburban street, the mountains on one side and the creek on the other, how she would turn the heads of the fathers driving past.

Lisette had moved away; her room had become the family room, with a TV stuck on CNN and books piled on the floor. Belinda passed it on her way to the kitchen, where she set down her bottle of wine on the counter. Jeremy was moving between the refrigerator and the sink, being domestic, and watching him she again felt the dissonance between this vision and the one she'd had of him in class. He was as focused on his chores as a housewife, scrubbing down the sink, spraying water at the plants on the sill, throwing out the wilted vegetables in the crisper. She recalled a morning earlier this summer when he'd brought her here while Deirdre was at work; while they talked he dusted, and she had watched in fascination as he nervously polished a tin of tuna before setting it back on the shelf.

"Can I help with anything?"

"No, I just have a few things to do here, and then I thought we'd sit out on the deck and have a drink. What would madam like to drink? There's whisky, gin . . ."

"I'll have a martini." Belinda grabbed her purse and went looking for the bathroom. The construction of the house was odd, meandering, with rooms opening out onto unexpected hallways. The downstairs bathroom was cramped as a closet. She remembered how at the party she had squeezed into the bathroom and stayed there for a long time, intoxicated by the green-apple smell of the glycerine soap by the sink, and the musk smell of the towels—his hands, his face, here and here. She walked upstairs past his son's closed bedroom door. Mark was eighteen but had not yet, to his father's puzzlement, showed much interest in girls. He loved animals and wanted to become a veterinarian. In school photographs Belinda had seen of him, Mark appeared a gangly and good-natured teenager, the gap between his front teeth exposed by his goofy grin. The two children with their different personalities seemed examples of nature, not nurture. Belinda wondered sometimes why she herself was the way she was, if somewhere in her genes it was predetermined that she would end up here, with Jeremy, like this.

She found her way to the upstairs bathroom, which looked lived-in and untidy—a shrivelled brown spider lay in a dusty web in a corner of the windowsill, and a few of Deirdre's grey-brown hairs were scattered on the bath mat. This little room seemed more intimate than a bedroom. Belinda flushed the cardboard tampon tube but, with a confused intent, slipped the Tampax paper wrapper into the empty wastebasket. As she washed her hands she glanced down at it, crisp and visible, blue letters on white paper. Undoubtedly Jeremy would see it and have the foresight to empty the basket before his wife's return. Then again, perhaps not.

"This dog is just going crazy," Jeremy said when she returned to the living room. He was bent over the record player, propping the needle up with a forefinger while lifting a record out of its paper sleeve. To Belinda, the bulky record player with its plastic lid like a cake cover was a relic from the past, an archeological artifact. Shostakovich's Piano Trio No. 2 swayed through the room. "I was hoping to wait till after dinner, but Toby's been cooped up all day and he'll just bother us if I don't take him out for a quick walk now. Here's your drink, madam. Can you amuse yourself? I'll be back in a minute." He stood in the doorway, the leash wrapped around one hand, gazing at Belinda and smiling mistily. She thought that perhaps he was picturing her there on the sofa for good. Then something of his old remoteness returned. He added, in the hard, practical voice of the married man he was, "If the phone rings, *don't answer it.*" Did he think she was stupid? She felt a brief flare of anger at him. Then he patted his thigh, the dog leapt in front of him for the door, and he was gone.

Belinda stayed seated, looking around her, breathing in the smell of the domestic intellectual household. Clutter and dust, classical records and faded carpets, wooden bookshelves splintering at their sides from the weight of their contents. The sunlight filtering in through the French doors that led to the deck captured a cloud of dust motes suspended in the air. There were photographs of his family on side tables and lining the shelves—his son and daughter as children, as adolescents with braces on their teeth, on graduation day. There were photos of Deirdre, which Belinda had picked up to examine on previous visits. She was an unremarkable-looking middle-aged woman, with a plump face and a rectangular body. There were chunks of grey in her brown curls and when she smiled for the camera it was a soft, lopsided grin. She looked like any number of suburban wives.

Belinda took another sip of her martini, feeling giddy. A sweet light-headedness swept through her, the first warning sign. She was hypoglycemic, and had stupidly skipped lunch that day. The dizziness would increase, the small amount of alcohol enough to make her high, and then would follow the slippery slope—wandering concentration, mental fog, confusion, as though her synapses were failing to fire. If left longer, the dazed feeling would develop into a sudden, overwhelming rage, or an exhaustion so acute that she would stumble and fall down.

A bracelet on the table grabbed her attention. It was made of polished wood the colour of tiger's-eye. Belinda picked it up and pushed it onto her wrist. It was too large for her; Deirdre was thick-wristed, she knew now. It slid off and she turned it around in her fingers. It looked like it had been bought at a crafts fair and was not the sort of thing she would wear, but suddenly she wanted to slip it into her purse. Days or weeks from now Deirdre might inquire about her bracelet, and Jeremy might put two and two together and call Belinda, his voice embarrassed but of necessity firm. "You didn't happen to see a bracelet lying on the coffee table when you were here, by any chance?" What would she say? Surely it wasn't worth it. As a

child she had once stolen a chocolate bar from the neighbourhood grocery store, and penny candy occasionally, but she had
not felt the impulse since. Now it seized her.

There was scampering and barking at the front door, footsteps, then Jeremy's breathless "We're back!" Belinda tucked
the bracelet into her purse, which she nudged away from her on
the sofa.

They sat on the deck at the back of the house, drinking martinis. It was a pale autumn evening, the last rays of light filtering
down through the branches of the evergreens lining the spa-
cious backyard. The garden was his wife's domain, filled now
with the last of the season's roses, blowsy and drooping. Here,
Belinda felt Deirdre's presence. She was sitting on a wooden
deckchair with arms shaped like paddles. Next to her was a
green watering can with a spout. She listened to Jeremy impatiently as he talked, light-headed with hunger; the alcohol
made everything shiny and off-kilter.

Jeremy had been pontificating about a new psychology text
he was teaching, occasionally interrupting himself to stare at
her and exclaim, "Oh, you're here! You're really here!" in a
besotted way. She wondered why she was here, when it seemed
to her she no longer felt any desire for him. But his desire for
her was too powerful to resist; he adored her, looked upon her
as if she were his life's miracle. Belinda knew that Jeremy and

his wife had not had sex for the past ten years, a loveless decade, except for a year-long affair with a neighbour who had since moved away.

They sat in silence for a while. She snuck a glance at her watch; it was half past eight. Finally, to her relief, he stood up and headed for the barbecue. "We're having pork chops tonight. I hope that's all right. I made a salad that's in the fridge. Do you want another drink?"

"Oh, why not." Belinda drained her glass, and when she stood up to go inside the house, the deck, the sky, the yard went momentarily black. Her head orbited in the darkness. The dizziness took her breath, and when she opened her eyes everything was composed of thousands of crackling dots, like the picture on a television screen. But within seconds the world rearranged itself normally and she went inside, staggering against the door frame.

Watching Jeremy prepare dinner, she vacillated between the irritation of her hunger and a sexual desire fuelled by the alcohol. When he brushed past her to check on the barbecue, his hand lingering on her arm provoked a flash of the long-ago heat she had felt passing him in the university hallways. Now she giggled and vamped for him, thrusting out her hip and posing in the doorway with one arm stretched overhead.

"Oh, you're marvellous," he said, brightening. He reached for her, then merely patted her on the waist and excused himself when the telephone rang.

Belinda slumped against the doorjamb, drinking her martini and watching resentfully as he talked to his daughter on the kitchen phone. He had slung a dishcloth over one shoulder and his sleeves were rolled up. His thinning hair shone in patches of silver. "It was great fun, Liz," he said, telling her about his recent lecture gig at a university back east. "I do like the East Coast, they have such a different mentality there . . . Mm. And how's the boyfriend? Good. How's work? . . . I'm just preparing dinner here, leading the bachelor life while your mom's visiting Mark. Well, I miss you too, we'll have to get together soon. Listen, I bought sweatshirts from the university for all of you. Yours will be waiting here when you come by . . . Love you too."

Belinda watched him, struggling to hide the hurt she felt at his choosing to speak to his daughter rather than pay attention to her. So what that he had called her every day that he was in New York, and written her a long letter in two shades of ink—his pen had run out halfway—on the flight. "I keep feeling that somehow things will work out for you and me, and that feeling is breaking my heart," he scribbled. She pictured him writing on a notepad propped on the meal tray, his elbow occasionally bumping the passenger seated next to him, one hand steadying his plastic cup of ice water when the plane encountered a patch of turbulence so it would not spill, like copious tears, onto his letter. "But I can imagine how furious I would be at myself if I walked away from my family, only to have you walk away from me. Now we are somewhere over Kansas, or Colorado. I always hold you in my thoughts."

The letter had bored her; she scanned the cramped, spidery handwriting impatiently, and after a moment she let it slip into the wastepaper basket.

The pork chop was dry and stuck in her throat. She carved resolutely at the slab of beige meat, shaped like a continent. It was protein at least, and after the first few bites she felt herself returning to stability, felt the fog receding and her vision clearing. This was what the doctor had ordered, small meals of protein and vegetables as often as six times a day, to keep her blood sugar level consistent. But when it dropped it was candy and carbohydrates she craved, and the liquid sugar of alcohol.

Jeremy disregarded the food on his plate, instead staring at her with the spinny-eyed look of adoration that she detested. "Why did you let me touch you, that first time? Why did you sleep with me? What were you thinking? Had you been wanting to? I want to know what was going on inside you, I want to know everything about you."

"I don't know," she said, trying to hide her mounting exasperation. Not because I loved you, you old fool, she wanted to say, to see the light snap out of his eyes, his face drain and crumple. More than a year after she had dropped out of university she had seen Jeremy at a downtown lecture given by a psychiatrist from Boston, and at the reception afterwards she went up to him. They talked for a long time over plastic glasses of red wine, and then she'd asked him if he would give her a lift home. He was less remote now; she was no longer his student, her future no longer in his hands. The power structure had changed and with it, she found, the hold he once had over her. Nonetheless, in the dark interior of the Toyota parked outside her apartment building, she touched his arm again as she had flirtatiously throughout the evening, and he turned to her with searching eyes and bent to kiss her. It seemed to her now that it was at that moment—the headlights of passing cars streaking the windshield, his needy expression, his breath catching in his throat—the moment when it began for him, that any desire she had left for him was snuffed out.

And thus this summer had begun, and so also the letters, poems and faxes he sent her daily, waiting for her when she came home from her job at the clothing store. In his poetry he referred to her body as "a gleam of gold glimpsed through part-ed darkness." He anguished over his marriage, his children, his long-term intentions towards her. He told her repeatedly that he loved her, and once roused her utter disgust when, into her answering silence, he said with clenched teeth, "I know you love me too, even if you won't say it." He seemed terribly old-fashioned in the way he gawked at her nakedness—she believed him when he said he had slept with fewer than a dozen women in his life—and in his clumsy, eager lovemaking, as if he were a boy at the start of his sexual career, rather than a man caught in the physical limitations of its decline. Still, he was company for a time, until her next "real" boyfriend, and he was attractive to her when he got out of her bed to put on his Polo shirt and Dockers, his hair white and mussed, his eyes round and myopic without his glasses, to go home to his wife.

Now, concentrating on her dinner to avoid his hungry gaze, she knew their affair was going to end soon. He had begun trying to talk to Deirdre. Sooner or later he would foolishly tell his wife about her and make some sort of demand for a divorce. What if he were to show up on her doorstep, weighted down by an armload of books and clothes, to say he had been deposed from his home? The thought made her wince. No, she would have to close the door on him before that happened, to spare them both.

But she would miss being the centre of another person's attention. Belinda reflected on this as Jeremy continued talking, on and on, veering from the day's news to his courseload at the university to his miserable marriage. Even though it could be trying, it was not an easy thing to give up. When the telephone rang, it was usually him, calling just to hear her voice. Once, after an apparently wonderful day of lovemaking, Jeremy became distant. "Where have you gone to?" Belinda asked.

"I'm thinking about the last time Dee and I had sex. I've never been able to forget it. Things weren't going well for us, she was depressed, we fought all the time. That night she was on top, and I came too soon. She stayed on top of me and then she just started screaming that she couldn't feel anything, screaming at me." He stopped. Belinda could see that his eyes were damp, red-rimmed. "I was completely shaken."

"Did you ever try again after that?" she asked after a moment.

"Oh, a few times, but it never culminated in anything. I'd put my arms around her. When I put my hand on her cunt"— the word surprised Belinda with its harshness—"she'd shrink back, repulsed."

Belinda made a sympathetic noise in her throat, but inside she merely felt bleak. It all seemed so ugly, so hopeless, what happened between people. So inevitable that it was hardly worth feeling sorry about any more. She looked at her lover and it seemed to her then that he was small and pitiful, an aging man.

"I've never told anyone this," Jeremy was saying now, and the intensity of his voice brought her out of her reverie. He gazed at her over his cold, barely touched pork chop, and there was such pain in his face that she put her wineglass down. "But I feel I can tell you. I feel I can tell you anything, Belinda." He paused, and continued with difficulty. "Do you know that once I thought of killing my own wife, that I came this close?"

Belinda was surprised, but not shocked. This was just more of the ugliness and the hatred that grew up between people who had once loved each other, touched each other reverently, exchanged vows before their families and friends.

"We were out hiking one day, about five years ago, in the woods near the canyon up the road. It was a beautiful summer day, like today. I'll never forget it. She was ahead of me and we came out onto the edge of this cliff, with the valley and the trees spread out below. I came up panting behind her and it was just glorious, this view. I can't explain what came over me. I guess it was a culmination of all the fights we'd been having, and our total lack of a sex life, and my building frustration. And the way she kept telling me I'd been a disappointment." He rubbed his misting eyes under his glasses while Belinda watched him silently. "Forgive me, but I nearly pushed her off the cliff. I wanted to so badly I had to clasp my hands behind my back. I dug my nails into my palms until they bled, Belinda, that's how bad it was. And she didn't know anything. She was just standing there enjoying the view, she didn't know that all I had to do was push her and she'd be out of my life forever."

He drew a ragged breath. She was aware of the clock ticking in the kitchen, the distant padding of Toblerone's paws somewhere in the house, the darkness gathered in the yard outside.

"When we came home that day, I got stinking drunk. It seemed so bad that she *just didn't know.* Since then, I've thought of that moment a hundred times."

"And?" Belinda was curious.

"And sometimes I wish I had done it." Jeremy lifted the bottle of wine and held it up to the light, examining the several inches of liquid left at its bottom. He sighed, and smiled at her shakily. "Well, enough. Shall we finish this? Otherwise Deirdre will wonder where it came from, we're both beer drinkers typically." He poured the last drops into her glass. "There. That means you'll be married before the year's out, Miss Belinda."

After dinner they walked the dog together. It was entirely dark on the long, winding street outside his home, and quiet, the particular hushed silence of the suburbs that was so different from her downtown apartment where there were always cars passing outside, the occasional holler and bottles breaking somewhere in the night. Here there was only the liquid murmur of wind through aspens. The black sheet of sky was crammed with stars, and this was Cheever country.

Jeremy slowed his long stride to match hers. He put his arm around her and she reciprocated, so they walked this way like a long-married couple, jerked forward occasionally by the impatient dog. The road was blank beneath her feet in the dark. There was a certain thrill to walking like this in his neighbourhood, an illicitness like sex. She thought that if the world had any kind of moral order, if there was anyone at all overseeing the right and wrong of things, lights would be snapping on up and down the street, his neighbours would be coming out onto their porches and front lawns, they would point at Jeremy and Belinda in accusation. But there was only the panting dog, the rhythm of their steps, the shattered stars above.

When a car did turn a corner at the top of the road and sweep its headlights down the block, Belinda felt Jeremy's body go quiet beside her. "Uh-oh," he said, then, "Don't worry, the neighbours are on vacation," and he relaxed. She realized then that that was why he'd been able to call her so often in the evenings recently—he had gone over to his neighbours', to water their plants and collect their newspapers and call his girlfriend.

But they turned back after that. In the living room again, Belinda sat flipping the pages of a photo album while he made tea in the kitchen. "That whole first section, Deirdre was about the same age you are now," he called. She bent over the laminated pages, scrutinizing his wife as he'd once known her. She had been good-looking, with long chestnut hair and the sort of symmetrical features universally recognized to be attractive. Her limbs were lean and she wore no make-up. Belinda thought this other woman was more attractive then than she herself was now, and felt a strange stab of competitiveness.

"Ah, you found our wedding picture," Jeremy said, coming to sit beside her on the sofa. He shifted her purse aside and she cast a guilty glance at him, as if he could somehow detect the theft she had committed earlier. But he was looking down at the album open on her thighs, and his voice softened. "You know, we had to do that about four times before my father managed to capture it on film."

In the photograph Jeremy and Deirdre were feeding each

other pieces of their wedding cake. Jeremy wore a suit and looked young and studious with his horn-rimmed glasses and smooth skin. His wife had her hair twisted up and looked chic in a tailored cream suit. Belinda was mesmerized by the photograph: two strangers, a man and a woman in love.

"Well, that was another life," Jeremy said softly, as if reading her thoughts. "I don't know where those people went. Sometimes I like to think there must be some parallel universe where all our lives turned out differently, where right now we're living in completely different circumstances, with different people, because we took the other path. The old fork in the road." He bent closer to Belinda. She could smell his clean skin, and a trace of soap or detergent. He still smelled good to her, as he had when she stood next to his desk at school and furtively breathed him in while he bent over her essay. "Maybe in one of our lives you and I are married. How would you like it if I got divorced and asked you to marry me, hm? That would show you, wouldn't it? That would be calling your bluff."

She giggled nervously. He had guessed that much: nothing would make her less happy than if he left his wife for her, except for the small ego boost it would give her. And even then how could she be sure it was her, that she was special, instead of just an excuse to exit a marriage he had been looking to leave anyway? She could not imagine their life together, except that it might be as corrosive as his life with Deirdre. She would hate him, but it would be impossible to leave him. What if they went hiking one day and this time he could not restrain himself from pushing his wife off the edge of a cliff? Or, more likely, what if he simply stopped loving her—what if the heightened excitement he felt for her, which possibly passed as love, ended—and she became the woman in the wedding photo that another young woman compared herself to?

Belinda stifled a yawn as Jeremy embraced her. It was nearly eleven o'clock, and she was tired from the late dinner and the alcohol draining from her system. She noticed that when he bent to kiss her, he pursed his lips like a fussy old man.

"I should go, it's getting late."

"So soon? I was hoping . . ." He faltered. "I wanted to show you my yearbook. It's right here, it'll just take a minute." He was already up from the couch, rummaging on a shelf, and she sat back resigned.

He had graduated in the fifties, the same pale, earnest boy she'd seen in his wedding photograph. His yearbook was lavish with autographs and scrawled good wishes. It was no different from her own yearbook decades later, but for the photographs. In the fifties, the teenagers had looked much more like serious adults, with conservative hairstyles and scrubbed faces. The boys looked like characters in "Leave It to Beaver," and the girls looked like the Blue Bonnet girl on margarine tubs. Wholesome. In the photographs these students glowed, smiling forth from halos of photographic light.

"That was another life entirely," Jeremy murmured, watching

over her shoulder as she turned the pages. "But most mornings when I look in the mirror to shave I still expect to see the person I was then. Who is this impostor with his jowls and thin hair? I look five years older than I am."

"Not at all," she protested politely.

"Yes, I *do*. But still you came along. I never thought you'd want an old geezer like me." His eyes had gone soft. "Look, I'll drive you home shortly. Just come upstairs for a bit. Come on."

He pulled her up off the couch, and she went with him because it was easier than resisting. God, she was tired suddenly. She dreaded the thought of the long drive home, through the suburbs, over the bridge, all the way downtown. All she wanted to do was sleep. The alcohol in her system gave her a rocky feeling, like she was all pebbles and gravel inside. These days she was easily exhausted, her supply of energy burned off in a few bright tipsy moments which left the long shadow of depression in their wake. It was a Herculean effort to get out of bed in the morning, put on her make-up, go to work and cater to the whims of the rich women who came to the store, collecting armloads of designer clothes, each half her month's rent, to try on and discard in the change room. Often she wished she had stayed in university, finished her master's and gone on to her Ph.D., but halfway through her master's she realized she didn't have it in her. When she looked at the stacks of textbooks, the essays and exams she would have to write, a wave of defeat washed over her. The thought of going back to school now was overwhelming; besides, she was no different from the other sales staff, most of whom had their B.A.s and were just as stranded as she was. So she bowed and scraped while thin women wearing stacked heels rifled through the racks, Prada bags slung over their shoulders, chatting on cellular phones. "Darling," they called her, "sweetie, would you tell me if this *goes?*" Their husbands were grey-haired and glowering men, captains of industry, proud of their blonde wives with their shellacked faces. These men viewed love as an acquisition; Belinda could see the scales tipping back and forth in their eyes, the checks and balances. They were people who had somewhere along the way gone hard in an instant, or perhaps they were like that from the beginning. Hour after hour she stood under the halogen lights, greeting her regular customers by their first names, judging at a glance which of the browsers would become buyers, rearranging the merchandise, doing inventory, steaming the silk blouses in the back room, her feet pinched in their Charles Jourdans. And when at last it was time to go home, she did not even want to return phone calls; she just made herself a sandwich and ate it in front of a rerun of "Seinfeld" or "Friends."

Belinda grabbed her purse and followed Jeremy up the stairs to the bedroom he shared with Deirdre. Their room was the most attractive part of the house; it took up most of the second floor, and was panelled in fragrant cedar. It had high ceilings and tall slanted windows overlooking the garden. The windows, the wood and the space gave the room a vaguely church-like feel.

Belinda allowed Jeremy to lead her to the bed, which was soft and covered by a white duvet. She lay down, folding her arms under her head, and looking up at the ceiling. He sat at the foot of the bed, his thin legs crossed. His hair was white, his face mapped with lines. He does look older than his fifty-six years, she thought.

"Well, then," he said, gazing down at her with a triumphant look in his eyes. "Here you are again, in my bed. Lord knows I imagine you here often enough, when I wake, when I go to sleep."

She didn't feel much of anything, only blank and detached. Was this just another way of dealing with pain, after all? She glanced around the room. There were shelves full of books on architecture and history, a photograph of Deirdre wedged into the upper right-hand corner of the walnut dresser, stacks of coins on the bedside table.

"Lord, this room has a lot of memories," Jeremy mused. "I remember when we were going through the worst of it with Lisette, with the drugs and the running away and the terrible scenes. Once Dee was so upset that she slapped her, and Liz didn't forgive her for that for a long time. I remember one evening we were having some kind of argument, Liz came in here and she said, 'You know, who the hell are you to tell me anything. I bet you two haven't even fucked in years.' She was right, of course, and she didn't even know it."

Jeremy lowered his glasses onto the bridge of his nose,

massaging the frown lines between his eyebrows. Belinda peered at him through her lashes. Her eyelids were heavy and she was desperately tired. Tomorrow morning she had to work the early shift, then help to organize a trunk show later in the afternoon. Whatever compassion she felt for Jeremy was fading quickly. She wished she was in her own bed.

"I'm not proud of myself for what I did that day," he continued, looking past her and wincing.

"What did you do?"

"Well, I grabbed Liz by her wrists and forced her down to the floor, right in front of this bed. She was struggling, scared, she'd never seen this part of me before. I held her wrists so tightly I left bruises, and I said to her, 'This hurts, doesn't it? Well, this is how you've been making us feel.'" He shook his head. "I shouldn't have done it, but it got through to her, anyway. She was pretty meek after that, for a while. And eventually she outgrew whatever teenage phase she'd been going through, and she's just fine now."

Outside the tall windows, the suburbs were in darkness. The lamplight cast a honeyed glow over the cedar-panelled walls, and the room was warm. It appeared the house could withstand any storm. They were both quiet, and Belinda could feel Jeremy's attention shift from the past to the very real present, to her in his bed.

He stood up and crossed the hall to the bathroom. When he shut the door she rolled over and looked at the tidy stack of coins on the side table. There was perhaps twenty dollars there, and she reached out, a cramp stapling her stomach with tension, pinched up several dollars, and dropped them into her purse on the floor. They clattered against Deirdre's bracelet. Then she lay back on the pillow, staring up at the ceiling, feeling foolish but better, less cheated somehow. It was hardly anything, not enough to compensate for the way things had turned out, but it was better than nothing at all.

When Jeremy returned he contemplated her for a moment, his eyes watering. He put his hand on her thigh and she shuddered. It seemed a long time since she had been happy with anything. Perhaps the last time was those early days in university, when she stood blushing outside Jeremy's office door, when the world was lined with maple trees and possibilities. Now his arms slid under her and pressed her close. She could see her own face, suspended in the lenses of his glasses, and for a moment she did not feel so dizzy and lost, so anchorless.

IN THE DESERT

JOAN SAT IN the passenger seat of the station wagon, waiting for her husband to emerge from the impotency clinic. They were parked in a small lot shared by the surrounding buildings—a real estate office, a travel agency, the Men's Medical Center— which were identical single-storey brick bungalows with venet- ian blinds angled over their windows. The building into which Henry had disappeared five minutes ago was the most discreet of the three, the blinds in its waiting room sealed shut, a hedge bordering its property. They had had to drive up and down the avenue before finding this address, which they eventually came upon by accident; they swung into the parking lot to get their bearings, and she looked up and noticed the sign on the build- ing. It caught her eye—a small brass rectangle by the door, its engraved letters glinting sternly, like the signage on a law firm.

"Well, I guess this is it, then," Henry said, turning off the ignition and staring ahead of him, into the waiting room of the travel agency. Joan glimpsed a pair of imitation-leather chairs, the bouffant blonde hairdo of the middle-aged travel agent behind her desk, a poster of Hawaii with palm trees and aqua-marine water. She couldn't imagine that the agency did much business, since it was situated in a city most people wanted to travel to, not depart from. This city in the desert, surrounded by mountains that stayed brown year-round, with its golf courses and mineral springs and restaurants catering to leisure-suited retirees. This was paradise—Henry's idea of it, anyhow. Her idea of paradise was to be back at home, helping her drama students mount a new production, working out three times a week, trying to stay fit and young.

He smoothed out the newspaper ad on his thigh, scrutinizing it and then the sign on the clinic, as if hoping they might not match. The borders of the local newspaper were filled with these "men's health" ads, running alongside Ann Landers's column, the seniors' discount matinees, the self-congratulating photographs of the desert's wealthy elite in their wigs and black ties, their wrinkled faces leering into the camera as they awarded each other plaques for their charity work. Philanthropy was as much a rat race for these people now as selling the most real estate or making the Fortune 500 list had once been, that is, if their names weren't already Hearst or Guggenheim.

"You really don't have to do this," Joan said yet again.

"No, I want to." His voice was overly enthusiastic as he

reached out to squeeze her hand. She squeezed back, but had to suppress a little shudder of revulsion. He drew in a deep breath and slapped his thigh. "Anyway, we don't have to do anything. This is a consultation, that's all, I'll just be talking to a doctor about my—problem. They deal with this sort of thing all the time. It shouldn't take longer than twenty minutes. Are you sure you want to stay in the car? I'll have to leave the air-conditioning on."

"It's too hot to go for a walk." Whoever claimed that desert heat was bearable because it was "dry" heat didn't know what they were talking about, Joan thought. The other day she had headed for the shopping mall—as she did most days, for lack of anything else to do—and the hundred-degree heat out on the avenue was thick and sticky; it pricked her exposed arms and legs, like needles of rain. The brown palm trees lining the divide at the centre of the road rustled like parchment; she wondered that they did not spontaneously burst into flame.

"Suit yourself, hon. I'll be back in a few minutes." He leaned over to kiss her, and at the last instant she turned slightly so that his lips missed hers and brushed her cheek instead. She smelled mustard on his breath, from the sandwiches they had had for lunch, and noticed a spot of it on his cherry-coloured sports shirt. She thought of calling it to his attention, but didn't, knowing it would upset him so much he would be preoccupied with it for the rest of the day. When he was a boy, an elderly neighbour would walk around with food stains on his clothes—

"You can always tell what Mr. Smith had for lunch by what he's wearing," people said—and this had so disgusted Henry that he vowed he would never be old like his neighbour. But the reality was that he was seventy and his neighbour back then had probably been younger than Henry was now.

He opened the car door and a blast of hot desert air, moleculed with sand, washed into the car. He stretched one leg out onto the pavement and lifted himself from his seat with a loud, unconscious "Unh!" Joan winced, her fingers curling into her palm. Henry groaned all the time now, when he sat down heavily into a chair, as if all the weight in the world were upon him, or when he rose effortfully, hauling his bones and his flesh upright. "Uunnhh!" he'd grunt, from his very depths. It made Joan want to give him a shove or a slap, to shut him up, to make him stop inflicting himself on her the way he did, all the time, in these small ways. There was the way he constantly, ineptly whistled, or walked around the house, singing, "Doo doo, du-du-du-du-du-du," or, "Wah wah, wa-wa-wa-wa-wa-wa," over and over until Joan clenched her teeth so hard it would give her a headache. It was too much, and yet, after Doris had invaded their marriage, it was what there was.

She watched her husband trundle down the gravel path to the clinic. He was short, with stooping shoulders and a sagging belly. His varicosed legs were sunburned beneath his shorts. A few strands of dark hair, matted with perspiration, lay combed across his scalp. He disappeared into the building and Joan watched him go with a mixture of feelings, including pity and shame. The air-conditioning rushed softly around the car's interior, and outside the heat lay over everything in a blinding white layer.

They had met when Joan found a position at a school where Henry was the principal. She was thirty years old and had never been married; Henry was twenty years her senior. He was a capable but emotionally distant principal who did not have many friends among his staff. Their relationship and quick sub-sequent marriage surprised Joan as much as anyone else, but he was intimate with her in ways his stern, somewhat shy demeanour could not have belied. As a teacher she was his opposite—she loved her teenagers, their boundless energy, their insecure swagger, the shine in their eyes when she put them on the auditorium stage and they finally grasped a line of Shakespeare or recited a monologue to wild applause from their peers. When, after they'd been married for fifteen years, she had one day received a phone call from a woman named Doris telling her that she and Henry had secretly started seeing each other, Joan had been devastated. But ultimately he had chosen to stay with her. And they had spent too many years together for her to consider leaving. She kept working after Henry had taken his retirement, and it was only in the past two years that she had switched to on-call teaching, to accommodate his desire to have her around the house, and to spend winters with him in the desert.

Joan never told Henry how the desert bored her. Each day was as relentlessly blue-skyed and sun-baked as the last. If they left the windows of the apartment open at night, by morning a fine layer of sand would cover everything—the glass coffee table, the windowsill, their own bodies in bed. Each day did not vary much from the one before. Henry spent most of his time watching television, napping or paddling around in the pool of the complex. Many of the other residents were partially blind, deaf or suffering from Alzheimer's; they slumped in the poolside chairs, their canes rattling on the tiles from their tremors. One old woman never seemed to leave the hot tub; she was always there when Joan joined her husband, the water roiling and splashing around her leathery limbs, gazing in their general direction with cataract-coated eyes.

"Ooh, I think that must be Henry. And Joan, is it Joan? How are you today, dears? Another hot day!" She patted the surface of the water with her brown hands, the skin stretched shiny over her bones, wrinkling a smile up at them with her sunken mouth.

"Yes, it sure is hot," Henry would say, lowering himself into the water, a beatific smile spreading across his face. "Aaahhh. Couldn't be nicer. I love the heat. Aaahhh." He would close his eyes and tilt his face up to the burning sun. Surely Joan did not belong here, she was too young, why didn't the others notice? But then she glanced down at her own body, distorted under the churning water in the hot tub. Her legs appeared skinny and veined, the flesh loosening from the bone, like chicken that had been boiled too long. She looked quickly away. Around the pool a few yellow roses straggled up the fence, and the palm trees drooped in the heat. Other old people groped past with their walkers and canes; one old woman had her middle-aged retarded son jiggling along beside her, his fat belly flopping over his waistband. "Isn't this wonderful, Joanie?" Henry said, reaching for her hand without opening his eyes. The sun flashed off one of his gold-capped front teeth. "Hot weather, two golf tournaments on TV and my sweetheart by my side. A hard job, but someone's got to do it."

Joan escaped by going shopping on the afternoons they did not spend at the movie complex down the street, the popcorn-scented air and worn seats a welcome respite from the thick heat shimmering outside. There was consolation to be found in the cool department stores, the whisper of the escalators gliding up and down, the plush changing rooms, the sensuous slip of fabric between her fingers. Sometimes she bought something—a bright, low-cut dress, a tight T-shirt—thinking of how she wanted Henry to see her, with surprise and lust, as if she were not herself but a woman walking past him on the street. Then the uselessness of it would come over her like a wave of nausea or depression—the realization that she was becoming one of those middle-aged women who dressed like a twenty-year-old, displaying a dry, wrinkled cleavage and flabby upper arms. On the walk home she would crumple the item into her shoulder bag, and sneak it past him when she walked in the door. It was an unnecessary subterfuge; he would not have noticed anyway, slumped on the sofa in front of the perpetual golf game glowing greenly on television, his eyes barely flickering up to acknowledge her entry. She would drape the offending item on a hanger and shove it into the back of the closet, or return it the next day. Once she owned something it no longer had for her the allure it possessed on the store hanger, as something temptingly beyond her reach, silky with the promise of youth. As soon as she emerged from the change room, gave a nod to the hovering salesperson and proceeded to the sales desk with the item and her credit card, it began to lose its desirability, and once it was wrapped in tissue paper, slipped into a bag and handed over to her with a smile, it was worthless. It became part of the reality of her life. The moments of excitement and covetousness that actually made her heart race when she looked at herself in the mirror, clad in the new garment, vanished in an instant.

But the hours in the department stores did pass the time. There was no purpose to their days in the desert, and if she could galvanize herself into feeling some excitement about a new dress, some anxiety about its cost, then that was at least a sensation. Otherwise there was only the time in the pool, newspapers, television and long naps she succumbed to with Henry out of simple boredom and lassitude, weakening under the weight of the heat. It was impossible to go for walks beyond the short trek to the mall or the supermarket, and even then she had to arm herself against dehydration with a bottle of water, which after three blocks would turn warm in its plastic container.

In the evening she would make a light supper and they would eat it in front of the television, or they would socialize with Henry's friends, retired professionals who led similarly leisurely, directionless lives. The men played golf, joined domino clubs or tinkered with house repairs, if they had always fancied themselves handymen; the women watched soap operas, experimented with complicated recipes, knit clothes for their grandchildren. They went for dinner at each other's homes, or in restaurants where the women longingly eyed the desserts, cakes as big as hatboxes slowly turning behind glass, snowy with coconut flakes, peaks of whipping cream, cherries. "Sinful, sinful, sinful!" they'd breathe, leaning in for a rapturous look, shaking their heads and pulling themselves away with effort. Joan wondered why they still bothered practising this self-restraint. But she did it, too, out of habit.

Often by ten o'clock Henry would be yawning. At home he would pull his clothes off hastily by the side of the bed, leaving them piled on the floor, climb under the covers and fall instantly asleep. Joan lay on her side of the mattress, in the semi-darkness, looking at him. She was aware of the jab of a spring against the soft flesh of her hip, the creases of skin across her belly where perspiration gathered. He faced away from her when he slept, his shoulder raised, his bare, freckled back turned to her like a wall to keep her out. The bed was lumpy, the room hot, the sheets tangled around her knees. Unexpectedly, a line from a scriptwriting course she had once taken came to her: "Every protagonist has to have a nemesis." That was one of the rules, because without conflict there was no story. Looking over at Henry, his oily, surprisingly smooth skin, his thin, wretched hair, his flabby buttocks, her eyes felt hot with resentment. If she was the protagonist, as she had to be, since this was her story, then was he her nemesis? Or was it her own body, succumbing to the downward tug of time? The hot, heavy silence, his shallow breathing deepening into snores, said nothing.

Those were not the worst nights.

When he turned to her, when he began kissing her and sliding his hands down her body, it sometimes seemed to her that Doris was part of their lovemaking. Even after their affair, he would absent-mindedly refer to her in conversation, seeming not to notice how Joan flinched at the sound of the other woman's name. And he had become unable to have intercourse with Joan. It seemed to her now that when they had made love Doris's warm, breathing body was part of the darkness in the room. She might have been at the foot of the bed, watching, or crouched in a corner, humming to herself. Joan felt, increasingly, Henry's regret at choosing to stay with his wife, and his lingering feelings for Doris. She felt she was not making love only to him but to the plump blonde, whose large breasts and hefty behind eclipsed her own body, diminished it. The bed even sagged a bit in the middle, as if Doris slept between them every night after they each rolled over to their opposite sides.

One night he woke Joan, nudging her to the surface of consciousness. Sleepy, fumbling, she rubbed his neck, thinking he was worrying about something, but instead he took her hand and guided it to his erect penis. Automatically she inched down and took him tiredly into her mouth, wanting to ease whatever tension he felt, but he pulled her up to face him and she understood that he wanted to try to slip inside her. She lay back and panted encouragingly, but as soon as he mounted her he went soft. "I'm sorry," he sighed, and she felt terrible for him. Full of pity, she made a move to go down on him again, but he put a halting hand on her shoulder and said, awkwardly, "No, I don't need . . ." his words trailing off into the darkness. She lay next to him, sensing rather than seeing his blank face, his eyes open and staring at the ceiling. She felt sick with embarrassment for them both. She thought of how, recently, she had begun panting like a porn star whenever he readied himself between her legs, thinking it might excite him, and how she involuntarily shrank away from him when he touched her. She felt overwhelmed by a wave of bleakness, and wondered in how many bedrooms this same scenario was being enacted, night after night, until each couple, wrung of dignity and desire, made some silent, mutual pact to stop trying. When he again hovered over her, straining to keep his erection, she looked at the wall beyond his shoulder and wished herself far away from this, from Henry squinting down in frustration at his penis, shrivelled and small between them, so disobedient to his commands that he shouted, "God, Joanie, can't you find a way to get it in there somehow!" as if it were her fault. A tremor of revulsion ran through her body as her husband rubbed himself against her, his penis like a limp little fish trapped between them, while perspiration dripped from his forehead onto her face, salty as tears.

But his impotence was selective, connected, it seemed, to the sight of her face, the reality of who she was. He could still stay hard in her mouth, hard enough for an orgasm. And so she would lie despairingly between his legs in the silence, his hands pressed flat, palms down, on the mattress, his breath quickening as she slid him in and out of her mouth, then his gasped profanities as he flexed into her mouth, filling it with a teaspoon of liquid that tasted like glue or melted plastic. How had her life come to this pass? It seemed as long as he could not see her, he could function, and it was even better for him if they were out of the bed entirely, away from anything marital or intimate, it was best if he stood and she knelt in front of him like a slave girl in the middle of the afternoon, the ice-cream truck tinkling maniacally across the street. His watch, a gold Gucci Doris had given him as a token of her affection, its strap worn and its face scratched, ticked loudly in her ear as she tried to bring him quickly to orgasm. His thighs were still surprisingly hard and she gripped them, pretending she was with a younger man, his scrotum full and heavy in her palm, not Henry's deflated sac. His penis nudged up against her throat and she struggled to think peaceful thoughts so she would not gag, and invariably what washed across her mind and relaxed her finally was the image of the department stores on the palm-lined avenue, their racks of colourful clothing, their fragrant cosmetic counters, how it was there she experienced something—a giddiness, a tension that quickened her heartbeat and dampened her palms, a bold thrust of desire—that mimicked love, or perhaps better, infatuation.

One night when his snores woke her she tried to turn him over on his side. He was leaden in sleep, and as she prodded him, lifting one arm and trying to roll him over, she realized that what she actually wanted to do was push him out of the bed, out of the apartment, and out of her life. Instead she propped herself up on her elbow and looked down at his sleeping face. Saliva had dried in a crust at one corner of his lip; his cheeks were puffy, his forehead high and oily, and his nose trembled slightly with each breath. The snores continued sawing out of his open mouth. "I must be going through a bad spell," he had said earlier that evening, his eyes averted, patting her arm absently. "I never had any trouble before. You must remember, you and I used to have sex almost every night, even when we were fighting. Now I have to fantasize, and that doesn't always work. I just have zero desire." He did not seem to consider how his comments might wound her, so that she had to turn away to hide the tears rushing to her eyes. There must be something grotesque about her that the fitting-room mirrors did not reflect. She was so ugly that he had to think about someone else while he attempted to enter her; perhaps he fantasized about Doris, with her dour countenance and her pudgy, rectangular body. When Joan tried to picture what he might be thinking about behind his pink, oily forehead while rubbing his flaccid penis against her vulva, as if her warm, alive body was a blow-up doll's, she wanted to vomit.

In the morning she woke with her hands balled into fists, bathed in bleakness, listening to the sounds of the television coming from the living room through the half-closed door. He was eating breakfast and watching a nature show; she could hear the clink of the spoon against the enamel bowl, the slurp of milk. She hated all the sounds he made now.

"This is the sex life of the fruit fly . . . The male can mate five times a day, and the female only once in her lifetime. No wonder she's choosy. How can she tell if he's a dream date or a dud?"

Already the room was hot; a trickle of perspiration inched

down between her breasts. Through the curtains a blade of yellow sunlight penetrated the air. A tidal wave of hopelessness washed over her and she lay pressing herself into the mattress, feeling flattened by the weight of their life together, by the empty day ahead of them. When she heard the dishes clatter into the sink and the front door close, she summoned all her strength to go into the bathroom and brush her teeth. In the shower she rubbed the apple-scented gelatin soap over her body with distaste—it was the soap he had just used. In the humid air of the bathroom she could detect his bodily warmth and odour, his just-departed presence. A blood-flecked tissue lay in the wastepaper basket, along with a discarded length of dental floss like a steely white hair, and bits of peppery whisker. She recalled how, when she had been first in love with Henry, his odour was like a drug; she would hasten through her nighttime ablutions so she could slip under the covers next to him, surreptitiously sniffing his body as they cuddled. Now his smell was like a poisonous fog that enveloped her, from which she could not grope free.

She pulled on a pair of shorts and sat down to her own breakfast feeling shattered. She had not slept well, and everything felt wrong. The apartment itself looked jangly and splintered, the glass coffee table hotly reflecting a square of sunshine, the air-conditioning loudly clanking and chugging, the refrigerator buzzing, the pot of water for her egg bubbling to a raucous boil. The very fibres of the carpet seemed to bristle against her bare feet. Mercifully he had turned off the television—he liked to have it on all the time, and even if it was silent, its flickering picture had a magnetic pull on her, its presence always in the corner of her consciousness. Today there was only the newspaper left folded on the kitchen table, the dusty sunshine, the heat inching up outside. When she went to the door, opening it to test the temperature, the heat was like a vacuum sucking her out, heavy and powdery, the scent of eucalyptus flowering the air.

She ate her egg quickly, scanning the empty apartment, her heart pounding. He would not be back for an hour at least—he liked to go for a walk after breakfast—and she had become intent on searching the apartment for the pornography she felt certain he consumed. She had to understand what he was thinking when he tried to have sex with her, what words and images tumbled in his head, what threads of lusty thought he tried to grab on to and climb towards orgasm.

She put the dishes in the sink and stood in the living room, her hands on her hips, looking around. Quickly, so as not to think about it further, she went over to the sofa and turned over the seat cushions. She looked under the furniture and behind the maple wall unit; in the kitchen she opened every cupboard, pushing aside cans of pork and beans and applesauce, plastic shopping bags collected for use as garbage bags, coffee filters. These were the unlikely places, and she didn't expect to find anything other than crumbs and dust. In the bedroom she swung the mattress off the bed to look under it, got down on her knees to look under the bed itself, went through the items in his dresser drawers. Nothing. She knew there was nothing in the bathroom, and that left the walk-in closet, which was stacked high with boxes. Folders of financial documents, old notebooks, paperwork he'd kept from the high school . . . it was impossible to sift through it all, but she felt this was a logical hiding place. She rifled through several boxes, lifting up an old cowboy hat on a shelf to look underneath, pushed aside a pair of tennis shoes and a broken racket. Surely there was something shameful here, something important to him. If she found something perverse, perhaps she would then know it was not her fault, that it was something beyond any woman to satisfy unless she was paid to do so.

She stood in the doorway of the closet, on tiptoe, idly tapping her fingers against the wall, wary of the sound of footsteps on the stairs, a shadow falling across the window. The bed, covered with its crocheted blanket, was warm from the sunshine. Light fell on all the furniture in the room, exposing a thin layer of dust. She could wipe and dust everything now, and still by tomorrow it would be back, blown in from the desert. They liked to leave the door open in the evenings, the dark blue night outside glittering with an apronful of stars, the thump of teenagers playing basketball in the park across the street, a mother calling in Spanish for her children.

Still on tiptoe Joan began patting the closet's top shelves for something she couldn't see, and her fingertips touched upon the slick surface of a magazine. She knew it was important by the way it lay, face down, pushed to the very back of the shelf. She retrieved it, and when it lay face up in her hands she saw that it was exactly what some part of her had expected all along but not acknowledged.

The woman on the cover was wearing a black leather corset and spike heels. She had a tattoo on her collarbone, a thorny black rose, and what looked like a brand on one hip. A cat-o'-nine-tails curled out of her fist.

Joan took the magazine and lay down on Henry's side of the bed, opening it carefully so that when he looked at it next he would not be suspicious, but this was unnecessary. The pages were well-thumbed, crumpled and smudged. They all displayed photographs of sadomasochistic scenarios—a leather-clad woman whipping another woman who was blindfolded and chained to the wall, a dominatrix slapping and spitting in the face of a male slave who grovelled at her feet, a masked man wearing unbuttoned leather jeans who gripped the hair of a young woman, naked and handcuffed, who knelt sucking his penis. A cold hand clenched around Joan's heart. Who did Henry fancy himself in these scenes—the punishing sadist with the rock-hard penis or the crawling masochist begging for the slash of the whip? She was worldly, she knew this sort of pornography existed. But she could not bear to think of Henry hurrying into a sex store in broad daylight, a felt hat jammed low on his head, his familiarly furtive gaze darting left and right before he ducked inside. Contempt curdled in her stomach at the image of him scanning the racks of dildos and blow-up dolls, poring over the shelves of videotapes, fingering the rack of magazines until he found the one that lay in her hands. Why this one and not a hundred others? Then the hasty purchase, the brown paper bag, and maybe the extra breath he had to take before stepping out into the bright, exposing sunshine.

She lay on his side of the bed, her head on his pillow, his scalp's oils transmitting a faintly rancid odour to her nostrils. As she paged through the magazine she imagined herself as her husband, and it was as if she became him in that moment, and saw and felt everything through him. The box of Kleenex located conveniently on the bedside table, the coils of the mattress pressing up against his flesh. If the curtains were left open, he would have one ear cocked for the stumping step of his war vet neighbour on the stairs, but he would not want to interrupt his growing sexual excitement to get up and close them.

For a few moments she entered so completely his experience that she felt a twinge of excitement herself, some lingering fierce desire to join with him in his most private self. But it passed quickly, and she rolled off the bed and stood on tiptoe to slide the magazine, cover down, back to its secret place in the closet. She nudged it away from her on the shelf with the tips of her fingers, as if it was something loathesome.

After that Joan watched him closely, and saw that he still experienced lust, though not for her and not for conventionally attractive women. The desert city, with its median age of sixty, was not full of opportunities to ogle women, but the ones who caught his eye were of a type—women like Doris, thick-waisted and heavy-thighed, with sullen, sulky faces and blonde hair. They wore blue jeans and no make-up and had a rough look about them, like they cared nothing for how they appeared to men. This was extraordinary to Joan, and impossible to accept. These were women who would never find sanctuary in the cool department stores with their gleaming milky floors and manicured saleswomen. Yet from the corner of her eye she would note his distracted gaze as they walked past, how his eyes followed such women sneakily, his broken concentration and the live-wire tensing of his body. Did he fantasize that these women wanted him, his complaining old man's body? Did he fantasize about his penis disappearing between such a woman's cottage cheese–dimpled thighs, his arms clasping her mound of a belly and her sloppy breasts fallen to each side of her chest? Joan felt a sour disgust rising in her throat; she could taste bile as they walked down the impossibly sunny avenues, his hand holding hers so unpleasant to her that her jaw hardened into rock.

One morning when she emerged from the shower she found him sitting fully dressed on the sofa, frowning at a piece of newsprint he had torn out of the paper. He looked up at her approach, and when she passed him he touched the side of her hip tentatively.

"Here," he said, showing her the ad. The newsprint shook a little between his fingers, and he raised his eyes to hers with effort. Their gaze briefly connected, then he looked past her shoulder and reached up to tweak his moustache, a nervous habit he had. He rubbed one glazed end of it over and over so that crumbs of wax and brittle ends of moustache hair came off between his fingers; unconsciously, he then flicked these onto the floor. "This sounds like it's legitimate. I think we should look into it. They might be able to figure out what's causing this thing. I mean, it might be as simple as a testosterone patch," he said, his words coming in a rush now. "I really don't think it's psychological or anything. It can probably be cured with some pills or something."

Joan looked down at the ad and stifled a bubble of hysteria that welled up in her. The awfulness of their situation overcame her; there seemed no end to the degradation they would have to endure. When she was able to look at him, his gaze still wavering self-consciously beyond her right shoulder, the pity that she felt for him, which might also be pity for herself, swept through her just as if it was love. Somewhere in there, it seemed, there was still a desire to protect him, a softness and a kindness that surprised her.

"You don't have to do this," she said, to help him.

"But I think it's a good idea. No, Joanie, I want to," he said, taking her hand and squeezing it. Finally he looked her in the eye and spoke pleadingly; the corners of his lips trembled with what looked like love. "Not for me, it's not so important. But for you. I want you to be happy. I want to do it for you."

Now it was Joan's turn to break his stare and look past him, out the window at the sunshine beating down on the brown lawn of the complex. She considered him approaching her in the dark bedroom, his chest covered with tangled white hair, a stout erection poking out between his thighs. She pictured him labouring above her, his jowls shaking with his thrusts, her gasps fake to her own ears, and distant, as if she was quite far away. For her? This was for her? She could not imagine that this was what she wanted; it was obscene.

Joan watched her husband as he emerged from the Men's Medical Center. The heat gave the outline of his body a shimmering quality; it made him appear warped, disfigured, so that she blinked. But it was only him. As he approached the car he glanced quickly left and right, as if people might suddenly leap out from the bushes, point at him and shriek with laughter. Was that how he looked coming out of a sex shop?

He hurried to the car, and when he got in he immediately slipped the key into the ignition. "Well, that was a bit of an anticlimax," he said as they pulled out of the parking lot, the black tar like melting licorice under the sunshine. "The doctor wasn't even in."

"You're joking." Joan had been ambivalent about coming here, but now she felt herself collapse inward in defeat. If nothing was done, then nothing would ever be done, and the nights would continue as they had until they simply stopped, until there wasn't even humiliation, but only emptiness. She doubted either of them could make this journey again.

"The nurse said he'd tried to call us earlier, at the apartment, to say he wouldn't be in. He had the flu or something. The answering machine must have been turned off. I ended up talking to the nurse instead. She asked me some questions, gave me these brochures"—he pulled some pamphlets out of his shirt pocket—"and suggested I call back tomorrow to book another appointment with the doctor."

She spread the brochures out in her lap. They all had similar cover photographs, of a strikingly handsome couple in their sixties, the sort of husband and wife who owned a boat or a summer home, who went on cruises to the Caribbean and instructed a gardener on the landscaping of their lawn, who drove a Lexus or Mercedes, whose children were university educated and successful in the professions. They had sleek silver hair and big teeth. They wore crew-neck sweaters knotted around their shoulders, sporty shirts with little horses on them, and their wedding rings gleamed prominently on their fingers.

Joan opened the brochures skeptically. The language inside was polite yet frank, printed in blue ink on glossy white paper, and there were small drawings of a penis in various stages of flaccidity and arousal. With an increasing sense of detachment she read about a procedure in which a man, ready mentally if not physically for sex, excused himself during foreplay to go into the bathroom, gave himself an injection, vigorously rolled his penis between his palms for several minutes until an erection was achieved, then re-entered the bedroom to ravage the lusty female who, unfortunately, could have a list of minor complaints after intercourse with the artificially stimulated penis, including vaginal itching and burning.

Joan sneaked a glance at her husband's mild, ungiving profile as he drove, his eyes straight ahead, the corners of his mouth downturned, his plump knees pressed close together, like a demure girl. She felt what by now was a familiar rush of pity and hatred, so that she had to close her eyes tightly for a second and then look out the window. The desert shook and blurred through a film of angry tears. The wide, forlorn streets, the mountains dry and brown against the brash blue sky, the banks of bougainvillea in Easter pinks and purples, the passing Rolls-Royces and Bentleys housing their octogenarian drivers and passengers, the wilting palm trees, the strip malls like air-conditioned space stations in the middle of this strange, desiccated city . . . There was nothing here. She tried to picture Henry in the bathroom that smelled unfortunately of the urine he kept spraying around the base of the toilet, standing with his shoulders slumped attentively forward, earnestly rolling his penis back and forth between his palms. The worst thing wasn't that she couldn't see it, it was that she *could*—she could easily imagine him in that humiliating circumstance, which would come as natural to him as any other.

She thought of a trip they had recently taken to Las Vegas for their twentieth wedding anniversary. There was a convention in town, and they went from one hotel to another, looking for a room. For a treat, because she had been so patient in the weltering heat, he rented a room on one of the top floors of the Luxor, the Egyptian pyramid with slippery glass sides and a beam of light that thrust phallically into the heavens, so bright it could be seen from space. That night, as he stood by the window overlooking the glitter of the strip, she knelt in front of him. The well-appointed room was silent as she laboured, a rasp of feeling in her chest, shame and frustration to say the least. His body was marble-white in the cloaking darkness, and his silence as threatening as a stranger's. For a long time she felt as if she was kneeling before a statue, inanimate and unyielding. She wondered what he was thinking of as he looked down upon the lights of Las Vegas. She let out a moan that he might have construed as her ardent feeling for him, the uncommon pleasure he thought she took in caressing him with her mouth.

After a while he touched her on the shoulder, a tentative touch, but with a commanding force behind it. "Move onto the bed," he said hoarsely. She obeyed, glancing back to see his outline against the steeply slanted windows of the room, his slumped shoulders, his sagging behind and veined legs, the tangle of old hair ruffling his chest, his stomach nearly hiding his genitals. His dark outline approached her like a threat, and when he pressed himself against her she was surprised to find him rock-hard.

"Can you fit *that* into you?" he sneered. She was unaroused to begin with, and his words were so callous that she felt herself close up entirely. When he tried to enter her it must have been like nudging up against a wall, so that he instantly went soft. He stood up in frustration, handling his penis roughly and mumbling. The shame descended around them again, like a fog; each unsuccessful attempt thickened it further.

Now Joan laid the brochures face down on the dashboard, with a sob that she quickly stifled by swallowing and coughing.

"Are you all right, honey?" Henry lifted a hand from the wheel and placed it over hers. She endured it, his gentle dry touch. "Do you want to get something to eat?"

She shook her head; he patted her hand and faced the road again. So that he would not see her tears she kept her face turned to the window, as if she was taking in the view. By the time they arrived back at the complex she had a headache from her contracted neck muscles. She went to lie down while Henry took the brochures from the clinic into the living room, turned on the television and flipped to the golf channel. Through the muffled throb of her headache she heard him scratch and sigh on the sofa, rustle through the day's newspaper, crunch and slurp his way through his favourite snack, a sugar-free chocolate-coated ice-cream bar.

Why, he'll live forever, she thought suddenly. He will live on and on, and I will grow old.

BLUE SKIES

"DELIGHTED," THE MAN wearing the three-piece suit murmured, "absolutely delighted to make your acquaintance." He held Becky's hand in his and manoeuvred her away from the group of men he was standing with, nodding left and right as they said their goodbyes. "Give my best to Annabelle," they said, and he took his cigarette from between his lips and dipped his head. "I most certainly will. Very kind of you," still pressing Becky's hand, coaxingly, as though he were leading her onto a dance floor. He turned his attention to her then, considering her with sharp blue eyes that seemed to miss nothing. A tiny smile played around his mouth. "I am sorry. Now, what was it that you said you do?"

It was the night of the opening of the new library downtown. Where, in a few days, book-clutching students intent on their research would crowd around the computer terminals, men in tuxedos and women wreathed in silk and perfume now stood, drinking champagne and eating sushi. Opera swelled from the glitter-strewn atrium, and further below, the children's literature section had been transformed into a wonderland of confectionaries, cakes and chocolates and sugar-spun castles. The guests were politicians, media, members of the arts and business communities. From a distant height they would have appeared like the variegated crystals inside a kaleidoscope, swirling together and apart in complex, shifting patterns.

Becky was invited because she wrote an entertainment column for one of the local papers. Early in the evening she had encountered, among the editors and journalists she knew, a local radio broadcaster and his wife who had lived in the city for many years and knew everyone. They swept her along with them through the library—"Walk and talk, walk and talk," Howard encouraged with a bemused smile—introducing her to gossip columnists, jewellery designers wearing their own sparkling creations, women whom Howard's wife Georgia ran to squealing for hugs and kisses. It was upstairs in the business section that Howard and Georgia introduced her to a group of cigarette-smoking, grey-haired men. One of them was Warner Maclean. Becky recognized his name when Howard asked after his wife, Annabelle.

Annabelle Blair. It was page-three news in the national papers when, after leaving a dinner party, Annabelle and her former husband got into their car and Reginald, who was drunk, drove them off the highway. Annabelle escaped with cuts and bruis-es, but her husband was killed instantly. Becky, like everyone else who heard the story, was shocked, sorry and, on some deep-er, shameful level, appeased. So even the rich had their prob-lems, and came to bad ends. But it was the photograph accom-panying the article that seized Becky's attention. Annabelle Blair standing tall by her husband's grave, the model of compo-sure, a woman who was stylish even in grief.

On a trip to Toronto to cover the film festival she had heard that Annabelle was remarried. "A fascinating man. Pity they're on holiday or they would have been here tonight. He'd have loved you and you'd have loved him," a producer told Becky as she accepted another glass of wine.

So she had known who Warner Maclean was when Howard had shaken his hand and asked after Annabelle. "She's still back East, she's joining me here next week. I'll be sure to give her your regards," Warner replied, and then smiled charmingly at Becky. He was not a handsome man—he was heavyset, with thin white hair and the breathlessness of the chain-smoking asthmatic—but he made her think of vintage wine cellars and fussing tailors, of sprawling estates with names rather than street addresses. His smile, together with the force of his gaze—trained upon Becky as though she was now the only person in the library, the only person of significance—gripped her. She was suddenly aware of her pulse, the heat of her own blood. Annabelle's new husband.

"And who is this lovely young woman, Howard? May I have the pleasure of making her acquaintance?"

His exaggerated, old-world courtliness seemed neither out of place nor pretentious. He seemed the sort of man for whom rules were bent, who was forgiven by women he betrayed.

Then he was holding her hand and leading her away from Howard and Georgia. As they talked Becky felt dizzy. Warner was an elliptical conversationalist, asking more questions than he answered; what he revealed of his past was only a glimpse behind a thick curtain of history and secrets. "I do many things," he smiled when she asked about his work. "Business, finance, corporate law . . . I've played many roles. I just acquired a company here in town, that's why I'll be here for a while, setting it up. I'm ready for some fresh air. Would you care to join me outside?"

They passed Howard and Georgia on their way to the escalator. Warner kept his hand on Becky's arm. "We will be stepping outside for a breath of air."

Howard and Georgia glanced at each other; Georgia raised her eyebrows, and dismay seemed to flash across Howard's face. "I see you've made each other's acquaintance. Well," he said, hugging Becky goodbye, "Georgia and I are off soon anyway. Goodnight, then."

Becky wondered how often they had seen Warner leave a party with someone other than Annabelle. But she felt open to anything. She thought of Annabelle's long, slender figure, her waterfall of red hair, and she accompanied her husband down the escalator.

They walked together through the atrium, outside. It was nearly midnight, and the high point of the party had passed. The floor was strewn with shiny foil stars, and the crowd had thinned to small groups huddled in the vast space, saying their last farewells. "What an event for this city," Warner murmured. The glass doors opened and downtown lay ahead of them, the whisper of traffic, the yellow streaks of passing taxis, the ghostly square in front of the library where a few benches were scattered.

"I need your help," he said once they were seated. He was struggling to light his cigarette with a heavy gold lighter. "This wind. I need your hands."

Becky cupped her hands around his mouth as he bent over, inhaling; the wavering flame danced in the lenses of his spectacles. It took several efforts, their hands touching, his breath warm on her palms; a prelude to intimacy.

"There." He leaned back, contemplating the arches and columns of the new library before them. "What a beautiful city this is. I'm looking forward to my time here. The company I just bought needs a lot of attention, but it's a challenge, and I like challenges."

"How long will you be staying here?"

"That depends. Nothing is certain. We'll eventually buy a house, but in the meantime Annabelle will be exploring her options, and I want to see about some other ventures, too. I'll be travelling back and forth for the first few months. You'll meet Annabelle when she's in town. I'd like to bring the two of you together."

Becky had her first clue that what he wanted from her was not what she first thought. He did want something, there was a hunger there, she recognized it. He hadn't always been wealthy; he'd been too eager to tell her about his current home—Cardinal, a mansion on a fifty-acre estate—and he was like a child showing off his toys when he let her weigh his expensive lighter in her hand.

"So, darling, what are your goals? What do you want to have happen in your life?" Warner inquired, exhaling a plume of smoke into the cooling night air. They watched the last couples leave the reception, hurrying to hail taxis or heading down the street to their cars, their heels echoing on the pavement.

"Well, I want my column to have some influence on this city, of course," Becky said, feeling herself drawn along by his questions, as though they were commands. "I just bought a one-bedroom condo which I haven't even moved into yet, but I'm already thinking about how much I want to pay off my mortgage and buy a bigger apartment."

"Yes, it's ridiculous—one bedroom! You should buy something magnificent, get into debt for a million dollars, see what that feels like. If you're going to be in debt, you should be in debt for a respectable sum, at least."

Becky was giggling. "So what are your goals? What do you want out of your life?"

"My dear, I want to die in my mansion when I'm eighty-eight, with my beautiful twenty-five-year-old wife weeping by my bedside." He smiled impishly at Becky, who herself was twenty-five. It seemed absolutely certain to her that that would be his fate. But at the same time she noted with interest that he hadn't included Annabelle in his vision of the future.

They continued to talk on the bench until the clean-up crew had carted the bouquets and balloons out of the library atrium. Warner kept surprising her with what he knew of the city's arts scene—the writers he had read, the painters and actors and filmmakers he had met—and impressing her with his curiousity about up-and-comers. He had travelled the world, made and lost fortunes in the stock market. When Becky glanced at her watch and saw that it was past two in the morning she stifled a yawn, but Warner was not in the least tired. "I only sleep three hours a night anyhow," he claimed. "The evening's just begun for me! But you're tired, you need your beauty sleep. Tsk, you're just a child and I'm already out-doing you. Come, let's find a taxi."

They rode the taxi through the still, silvery streets to Becky's apartment. "Well, I enjoyed our conversation," she said as she climbed out and stood in the street under the horse chestnut trees, aware of him watching her from the dark interior of the cab. His eyes rested on her legs, travelled up her body, met her gaze. Although she was wearing heels, stockings and an alluring dress, she knew she was no match for Annabelle, and she looked back at him defiantly. If she had any advantage, it was youth.

"It was nice meeting you." She pulled her keys from her purse, started closing the car door.

"Yes. Wait, let me give you my number," he said hastily. "I'll give you the number at the company, since we haven't settled down anywhere in town yet. It's easiest to reach me there. And is there a number where I can reach you? Annabelle and I may wish to invite you to something when she's in town."

Becky had had affairs with married men before. She was wise to men who gave her their numbers at work but not at home. Yet Warner Maclean seemed sincere about including his wife in any relationship they might have, and this was no less intriguing to her, somehow no less edged with potential.

At the gym the next morning, while she was on the Stairmaster, Becky waved to an acquaintance. Rachel was the business reporter for another newspaper in town; they had struck up a conversation one day in the locker room of the health club and then realized they were both journalists. Becky had seen her last night at the library opening and at first failed to recognize her wearing make-up and an elegant silk dress instead of a T-shirt and sweatpants.

In the locker room, among the other women jostling for

bench space, Rachel grabbed her arm. "So I see you've met Warner Maclean. Interesting man, isn't he? I'm scheduled to do a profile on him, and I'm supposed to be following his progress at his new company. What did you think of him?"

Becky didn't know the other woman well enough to say. "I liked him. He was interesting to talk to."

Rachel eyed her. "He's a fascinating man, a real character. Did I see you leaving together last night?" she ventured.

"We just sat outside and talked for a while."

"Well, you've heard about his wife, Annabelle? She's set for life, at least. I heard from a reliable source that Reg Blair left her very well off." Rachel rolled her eyes. "She doesn't have to worry about making deadlines and trying to write interesting articles about some company's annual stock reports, like I do. Well, gotta go," she said, pulling up the hood of her nylon jacket and grabbing her gym bag. "Do let me know how things go with Warner!"

Becky laughed then, because Rachel looked over her shoulder as she swept out the door and gave her a parting, lascivious wink.

Several days later, Warner called. It was a Friday evening and Becky was having a small dinner party—her last in her old apartment. Her guests, a young married couple and one of her girlfriends, had brought champagne to celebrate her new status as homeowner. When the phone rang it was past eleven and her married friends were arguing bitterly while her girlfriend was praising Becky's burnt apple pie and murmuring, "Ah, married life. Now I remember why I got a divorce!"

"My dear." Warner's voice came over the line, and Becky's heartbeat quickened. "I had a wonderful time the other night at the library. I've been thinking about you since."

"I had a good time, too."

"What are you doing this moment? Would you care to join me for a late supper?"

"Actually, I have people over for dinner right now," Becky said.

"Well, let me leave you to your guests."

"No, that's okay. I'm glad you called."

"Listen, Annabelle will be in town on the weekend. Are you around then? I'll call you and we'll find some time to get together. How does that sound?"

On Sunday afternoon Becky arrived at the downtown apartment building where Warner and Annabelle were renting the penthouse floor. The elevator doors opened to the swelling notes of Beethoven's Ninth Symphony filling the hallway; she followed the music to its source, an open door flanked with potted palms, and walked inside.

"Hello?"

No one answered, so she stood in the foyer and looked

around. It was a magnificent apartment, which filled the entire upper floor of the building. There was a sunken living room, vaulted ceilings, floor-to-ceiling windows that ran the length of the suite. Silver light splashed from skylights onto the white marble floor. The source of the music, a complex wall of stereo equipment, was situated by a dining-room table set for a party of twelve. Linen, silverware, crystal glasses—all that was missing were the guests themselves. Something about the laden dinner table bereft of food or company struck her as poignant, and a little sad.

"Darling," Warner said, approaching her suddenly from one of the many doorways that led to a series of hallways and other rooms. He was nattily attired in a velvet smoking jacket and tweed trousers, and Becky felt as if she'd committed a grave sartorial error in her baggy sweater and leggings. "How are you, darling. Welcome." He took her hand between his and kissed her on both cheeks. She closed her eyes and breathed him in. His smell, of tobacco and fine fabrics, soothed her. He drew back and smiled at her in the knowing, observant way she was coming to recognize. It made her feel naked before him, as if her thoughts were written plainly on her face, and though this was disconcerting it didn't frighten her the way she might have expected. "Annabelle's just getting dressed, she'll be out in a while. She sends her apologies. We were having a little nap. Come, it's a lovely afternoon, let's sit out on the deck and have a drink. What can I get you to drink? I know, I'll make what we have when we're on vacation, you'll like it, rum and fresh juice . . ."

He wandered into the kitchen and Becky opened the sliding doors to the deck which circled the building. It was a pleasant day made beautiful by the height and panoramic view. The clouds in the blue sky were faintly pink-cast. The city below was mountain and architecture, forest and ocean. She wondered what it would be like to live like this. To feel you deserved so much in life. Would there be any room left for fear?

She turned around at the sound of a woman's heels on the marble floor. It was Annabelle, older, but more beautiful than her photograph suggested. She extended her long arms, folding her guest in a cool embrace. "Welcome, welcome. Warner speaks so fondly of you. Lovely to meet you, my dear, how are you?"

"I'm fine," she managed to say, intimidated by Annabelle's elegance. "You have a wonderful place here."

Annabelle smiled. Becky could see the deep lines in her face, which only seemed to emphasize her beauty, as if when she was young her face had been a painting, whereas now it was a sculpture. Her red hair swept past her shoulders; she was wearing a silk blazer the colour of Kraft caramels, linen pants and high heels.

"Well, let me show you around, then. Warner, are you fixing drinks? Good. Come, follow me, ignore the mess. It's insane right now, we're so unsettled, flying back and forth between our houses . . ." Her voice was sultry, perfectly modulated.

Becky followed her through the convoluted suite, looking at her as much as at the surroundings to which she gestured, swivelling her arms like Vanna White. They passed through a series of elegantly furnished rooms, and when they hurried past a dressing area with lit mirrors and piled clothes, Annabelle giggled, waved her arms in the air and exclaimed, "Ooh, what a mess! And the house isn't being cleaned until tomorrow! You don't see this, you don't see this!" Becky could picture her as a young girl hosting a pyjama party—the same giggle, the flirty movements of her hips and hands.

After the tour they joined Warner on the deck with their drinks. "I'm looking forward to us becoming better acquainted," Annabelle said, smiling invitingly. There was something arresting about her smile that Becky couldn't quite describe to herself. It was oddly sexual; her lips would part and her tongue seem to meet the roof of her mouth, as if she were holding a candy there whose taste she was savouring. "Warner called me the day after the library opening and said he'd spent half the night talking to a young woman there. He said you were most interesting. 'Oh, really?' I said. 'I have to meet her!'"

He had clipped shades over his glasses and settled back into his deckchair. Annabelle smiled intimately in his direction, drawing deeply from the cigarette Warner lit for her. Her fingernails were long and shockingly red; they were incongruous with her conservative outfit, belonging instead to some gala evening she had recently attended. Her gold-and-diamond jewellery flashed, sunlight and ice, against her skin. Warner was watching the two women behind his dark glasses.

"Now, if you'll both excuse me for a minute, I have to make some phone calls," he said, heaving himself up from his chair. "You girls have much to talk about, I'm sure, so I'll leave you out here. Just call me if you want another drink."

Becky felt trapped, out on the deck alone with his wife. But the rest of their conversation revolved around the entertainment scene in the city—who was doing what, what had happened to whom, in the years that Annabelle had been away. She seemed interested that Howard had been the one to introduce Becky to Warner; they had known each other a long time. "I used to have a crush on him," Annabelle confided. "He's such a lovely person. But he was married at the time."

"Oh, I can relate to that. I've been in love with married men."

"Then you know. For most of my twenties, I was madly, self-destructively in love with a married man. Then I was married to a wonderful man, who died. He was everything. The love of my life. It nearly ended my world."

"Annabelle, telephone for you!" Warner called.

"Let's go inside. It's getting chilly," Annabelle said, rising.

Becky made to follow her inside but Warner came out onto the deck. "It's still lovely out, what is she saying," he said, carrying a tray of fresh drinks. He removed his shades and gazed at

Becky. They were alone, his wife was down in the living room on the telephone. He smiled at Becky and circled his arm around her waist. "Well, my dear," he murmured, and said nothing more, only kept looking into her face, the pressure of his arm steady around her. They stood like that for a long time until Annabelle called, "Warner, how are we for Tuesday evening?"

Becky followed him inside. She felt warm, blanketed by his embrace.

Afterwards they sat and talked for a while longer, but the light was going out of the sky and the first euphoric rush of their drinks had passed, leaving the gritty, dazed feeling that comes from drinking in the afternoon. After a while Annabelle yawned and looked at her husband. "What time is it, darling?"

Warner looked at his watch. "We should think about getting ready," he said.

"Forgive us, but we have an event to attend tonight," Annabelle explained. She ran her fingers through her hair, preened briefly at her reflection in the mirrored wall.

"Oh, I must go," Becky said hastily, thinking that she had overstayed her welcome. She was embarrassed; she still did not know what they wanted from her, what they expected.

Arm in arm, Warner and Annabelle walked her to the door. Annabelle kissed her again, pressed her close. Against her, Becky felt the excess of her own flesh. "It was so wonderful to meet you at last," Annabelle said.

"Yes, at last," Becky repeated.

Warner followed her out to the elevator. She stepped inside and turned to face him. He watched her intently, his head tilted to one side, until the doors began to close.

"I'll be in touch," he said.

Over the next few weeks Becky was busy preparing for her move and with finishing a cover story for a local magazine. In the chaos she did not have much time to dwell on her meeting with Warner and Annabelle. Warner called her several times, late at night, to talk; Annabelle was back East with her family, and he was calling from his office long after his employees had gone home.

"Maybe some evening I'll arrange to have you come and visit me at the office, if you like. But I'm afraid it wouldn't be very interesting for you. Just a lot of computers, a lot of people working. It's marvellous, though, when you think of all the work going on in this city. So much energy, so many different projects. The creative energy, the business energy, it's wonderful."

He was so upbeat that Becky did not think he was calling her out of loneliness, though she wondered about him going home alone to the rented penthouse suite after he left his office at two or three in the morning.

Becky moved into her new condo at the beginning of May. It was nicer than anything she had lived in before, and she owned it, but some mornings she would sit in the tiny living room with her cup of coffee, look around her and think of Warner and Annabelle's life. Then, what she had seemed inadequate, and she loved less the sunshine that came in through the south-facing windows, the cozy bedroom and pass-through kitchen than she had a moment before.

One night three days after she moved into her condo, he called. "What are you doing right now?"

"Actually, I'm sitting on the sofa in my bathrobe, reading a magazine."

"Ah, so young, and already leading the life of a sybarite. Put some clothes on and come down to my office, all right, darling? I'll show you around and we can go out for a drink, how's that?"

She could not suppress the anticipation that made her heart race as she dressed and hurried down to his office. His new company was situated in a building in the warehouse district, an area that was being gentrified into trendy lofts and restaurants that catered to film people and stockbrokers who drove flashy cars, dressed fashionably and who all, it seemed to Becky, had the same predatory look on their chiselled faces. It was past nine o'clock, and to enter the building she had to punch in a code. A young male voice came over the speaker.

"Yes?"

"Hi, I'm here to see Warner."

"Annabelle?"

Becky felt odd, being mistaken for his wife. "No, it's not Annabelle. I'm—a friend of Warner's."

"Oh, okay," the voice said uncertainly. "I'll buzz you in, come on up."

Becky went up a spiral staircase and down a corridor to Warner's company. The door opened onto a wide space filled with dozens of desks and computers. Several men in their twenties and thirties, with longish hair, wearing T-shirts and jeans, continued to labour over their computers. The one who had let her in stood up and gestured to her.

"You're here for Warner, right? Follow me. Mr. Maclean," he called, "you have a visitor!"

"Yes, of course. Rebecca, how are you, lovely to see you," Warner said from the doorway of his office. He was impeccably dressed in a black pinstripe suit, and he wore a white carnation in his buttonhole. His shoes were polished, and gold glimmered off his cuff links and on his tie-clip. Again Becky felt painfully gauche. She had put on a sweater and jeans, not wanting him to think she was dressing up for him as though she had mistaken their visit for a date. "I was just sitting here, reading and thinking. Meditating, really. I've been in meetings all day and it's time for a break."

"I like your office," she said, admiring the vast mahogany desk behind which he sat like a tycoon.

He laughed. "You should see my office at home. This is merely temporary. May I show you around?"

She followed him through a succession of boardrooms and offices filled with filing cabinets and boxes. Even as he explained it to her, she could not grasp exactly the nature of his business—something involving research and cutting-edge technology, the Internet and the World Wide Web. "We're just in the beginning stages of establishing this company and making it really vibrant," he said. "There's a lot of work to be done, but I'm confident I can get it off the ground. Look, isn't this wonderful?" He paused in front of one of the computers, where complex graphics danced across the screen. "The advances of technology. Marvellous. And look, there's the company logo." He beamed into the screen. "Shall we go for a drink?"

They walked through the warehouse district. It was a warm evening, and the outdoor patios of the restaurants were crowded with leggy young people, flirting and laughing. They found a bistro on a narrow street where they could sit outside and drink martinis.

"Oh, but this is wonderful," Warner said, lighting a cigarette. "Isn't this wonderful? Sitting outside on a lovely evening like this."

Becky wondered if he savoured everything, all the time. They talked for a while about their work and their travels. He mentioned the books and magazines he was reading, the plays and operas he had recently attended, the dinner parties given by famous people to which he was invited. He knew as much as she did of the local scene, if not more, though it was her job to know, not his. When she asked about his family he admitted it was overwhelming.

"I have family all over the place. Children from my first marriage, children from my second, grandchildren . . . nothing but family."

"How do you have time for all this?" She shook her head. "Your family, your marriage, travelling all over the place, starting a new company—I get tired just thinking about it."

"Well, those are all different lives, aren't they? There's the business life, the social life, the family life, the love life . . ." He counted them off on his fingers. "And the interior life, don't forget that. Most important of all, there's the interior life, which is private." He smiled at Becky. "Which is not for anyone to know."

"Not even your wife?"

"No."

When they rose from the table it was after one in the morning. The sound of laughter and tinkling glasses drifted towards them from the busier restaurants. Becky was drunk from the gin; he had had two martinis for her every one, but they seemed not to have affected him. Wordlessly, while they walked, Warner put his arm around her. He drew on his cigarette without looking at her, and they fell easily into step. It occurred to her that someone passing them in a car might think they were a couple, and this pleased her.

"My condo is just two blocks ahead. I've got more gin there, if you want to have another drink," she said. "Then you can make fun of how small my place is. That is, if you're not too tired."

"I'm never tired," he said, smiling sidelong at her. "I'm impervious to being tired. I'm impervious to heat, impervious to cold—some people would say I'm impervious to emotion, too."

"Are you?"

"Ah, who knows, darling, who knows."

He prowled around her condo, looking at the books on her shelf, the prints on her walls. He took off his suit jacket and she saw that he had a potbelly and a slight stoop. She would never have noticed him had it not been for his manner and his intellect. He continued to inspect her condo, wandering from room to room, then they ended up in her bedroom; he sat on her bed and she sat in an armchair, one leg folded up beneath her. It was very late and she felt tired but content. She liked the intimacy of him sitting where she slept. It seemed enough; she would be surprised if he wanted anything more.

"Darling, I must be going," he said suddenly. "I shouldn't be drinking like this, it's very bad for me."

While she went to fetch his jacket he stood at her living-room window, looking out. "Let me tell you something," he said, then paused. Outside was the darkened parking lot, the neighbouring high-rise where other young, working professionals watched television, ate dinner from take-out cartons on their sofas. "The most important thing I've learned is this: when it comes right down to it, all you have is yourself. Other things—money, lovers, friends—come and go. I've been incredibly wealthy, and I've been bankrupt. It doesn't matter. What you must never forget is that as long as you have yourself, that's enough."

Becky watched him. At that moment, framed against her dark window, he looked inexpressibly lonely. Then he turned and came towards her, and they kissed. He pulled away and looked at her, searchingly, then they kissed again. His lips were warm and she wished she could put her head on his shoulder, her face against the fine wool of his suit jacket, and go to sleep breathing him in.

She lay awake in bed for a while after he left. She recalled how earlier in the evening he had looked at her over his martini and said suddenly, out of the blue, "Do you think I will harm you? Do you think that I want to hurt you?"

"No," she'd answered, startled. "I don't think that. Why would you want to?"

"That's right." He considered her, his eyes opaque. "That's a very good question. Why would I want to, indeed."

"Are you up for dinner?" Warner asked, calling two weeks later while she was watching television. "I'll come by to pick you up. My meeting will be through at eight. Just a minute—yes, bring me those papers, sweetheart. *Those* papers. Sorry, Rebecca. Is eight-thirty all right? Good. I'll be by then."

She waited for him, dressed up for a change in a skirt and a linen jacket.

When he arrived, he was not ready to go for dinner. "There's one thing we must do first. There's a building down the block I've been thinking of buying. Let's go and have a quick look at it."

Becky wondered if he was trying to impress her. The building, a former warehouse, ran the length of the block itself. Together they examined the building front and back, walking through the alley while he pointed out its features. "I like the display windows, very open and airy. We'll get rid of those ugly canopies, though. And this docking area here, it should be very nice in the summer when it's fixed up, the employees can sit outside to eat lunch. Well, I like it. I'll make inquiries in the morning. Let's see, then, where shall we go for dinner?"

He took her to the best restaurant in town, where the hostess fussed over them, the owner emerged to pay his respects, and their waiter led them to "the most romantic table in the house." She was aware of her tense, rising excitement, as though they were living out a fantasy in which she was his mistress, or perhaps his wife. It was a late spring evening, and they settled into a shady corner of the terrace, below the chiaroscuro sky. Irises and tulips lined the veranda and the tables were set on terracotta tiles which, if it were raining, would make the terrace appear to be awash with blood. Umbrellas the colours of sorbet shaded the widely spaced tables where couples dined discretely.

"Ah, this is perfect," Warner sighed, settling into his seat. "Isn't this beautiful? I come here several nights a week when I'm in town. Do you like this place?"

"It's very nice. I've been here once before," she lied.

"Well, it's a treat for you, then. Good. The food here is spectacular. Shall we start with some carpaccio? You look very nice, by the way, although," he frowned, plucking at her sleeve, "your sleeves are too long. What you need is a tailor."

Becky laughed. "Where's Annabelle? Does she know we're out having dinner?"

"She'll know. I'll tell her. I don't keep secrets from my wife."

"Has it always been that way?"

"Oh, I had girlfriends when I was married in the past. Many girlfriends. Darling, you'd be shocked. At one time I was seeing three women at once, not including my wife. Lovely, very smart women. They've all remained good friends. But I never kept anything a secret, because that, you see, is what destroys everything. It's not the affairs, it's the secrets."

"What about now? Do you have girlfriends now?"

"No. Annabelle is more than I can handle." He chuckled softly. "It was important to her, before we got married, that I understand she would be the only woman I was with as long as we remained together. I accepted that because I fell in love the moment I saw her. It was at a reception back East. I was there with another woman, a girlfriend I'd had for many years, and that night I left her for Annabelle. I treated her badly, but I was in love."

Becky propped her chin in her hand and looked at him. "Will you be married to Annabelle forever?"

He smiled at her in a way that shrugged off her question and stared across the terrace, the tables like islands, the white-jacketed waiters gliding silently back and forth. "Hmm, forever. What's forever? What's a month, a year, a decade? Who knows."

At the end of the meal, over espresso, Warner said, "What's the matter, darling? You seem distracted. It's a lovely night. Smell the eucalyptus in the air. Yet you don't seem happy."

"I'm sorry." She had been thinking about the night they kissed, wondering if it had meant anything at all to him. "It is wonderful. You are, especially. I don't meet many people like you."

It was out before she could censor it; it sounded so gauche that she winced.

"Oh, you will." He smiled at her indulgently, as though she were a child. "There's lots of people like me around. The question is, is that a good thing?"

He signed for the bill and they rose from the table. On their way out of the restaurant she became aware of a clicking noise, metallic, musical; it appeared to be coming from the direction of his shoes.

"Oh, my God." She laughed. "Is that you? Do you have taps on your shoes?"

He grinned mischievously and tapped his shoes against the pavement.

The taxi swept them through the streets and before long they were at her door. He climbed out and walked arm in arm with her up to the front gate of the high-rise.

"I'm going back to the office now, there's an endless amount of work that needs to be done. It's crazy, the hours I've been working. I'll be out of town for the next few weeks, to be with Annabelle, so I won't be seeing you for a while, my dear."

Becky reached out to embrace him. He held her warmly; the heat of his body radiated through his clothes and enveloped her. She breathed him in. After a long moment he held her at arm's length and regarded her.

"You are a sweet thing. So young." He touched her cheek. "Now, behave while I'm gone. Keep a good head."

She nodded.

He smiled, not letting her go yet. His gaze was steady, holding hers like a cord of steel. "And a good heart. Most importantly, don't forget, keep a good heart."

His shoes tapped back down the stairs and towards the waiting taxi.

It was early summer when she next saw Warner and Annabelle, at an opening for a new exhibit of photographs by a local photographer. By then someone else had come into her life—Brian Thompson, a successful painter she interviewed for the paper. He was in his early forties, recently divorced, and lived in a simple house in the suburbs. He was sweet, reclusive, lacking the hard edge that drew her to men like Warner. But she was comforted by his attentions; in their lovemaking he was so gentle with her, as if she might break.

Alone at events like this, she missed Brian's reassuring presence. The gallery was packed, and she shouldered her way through the crowd to try to get a glimpse of the work on the walls.

"Darling," a familiar voice said, and a hand extended to clasp her arm. It was Warner. "Why don't you come to dinner with us? We're going to the place I took you before."

"Dinner with you?"

"Me, you and Annabelle," he enunciated. "She's here somewhere, talking to Howard and Georgia when I saw her last. Stay right here. I'll go find her and we'll go to dinner. She'll be thrilled to see you."

Becky quickly drank two glasses of wine while she waited for her dinner companions. She wondered at the way her heart had dropped in disappointment when Warner said that Annabelle would be joining them for dinner. Was she infatuated with him? She didn't know what she felt for Brian either, beyond a confusion of tenderness. Who or what did she want, and did any of this have to do with love?

"Becky, my dear. I'm so happy to see you again," Annabelle said, her face lit, emerging from the crowd with her arms outstretched. Becky stood reluctantly in her embrace; she avoided meeting the other woman's eyes when they drew apart.

As they were led to their table on the veranda of the restaurant, through an arbour of sweet-smelling flowers and vines, Becky caught glimpses of the three of them in a series of mirrors along the wall. Her own face appeared bloated, her lipstick a smudged gash of red across her mouth. Warner was impeccable as always, in a three-piece suit with a silk handkerchief folded into his breast pocket. Annabelle's hair lay softly on her shoulders, a cascade of red; she was wearing a narrow skirt, a sleeveless wraparound silk blouse, and Becky saw that her arms were freckled. As they proceeded to their table Becky, who was also wearing a skirt, briefly admired her own legs in the mirror. At least my legs look good, she thought. Too good . . . Then she realized she had mistaken Warner's wife, who was walking alongside her, for herself—she had mistaken Annabelle's legs for her own. As they passed the bar a group of men turned to look at Annabelle, and Becky decided this was an evening when she would get very drunk.

After they settled at their table and ordered, Becky excused herself to go to the bathroom. "I'll join you," Annabelle said, familiarly leading the way.

"Don't you love this place?" Annabelle called out. She was in front of the sink, extracting cosmetics from her purse; Becky heard the brush stroking through her hair, the click of a compact snapping open and closed. "Such beautiful people come here. Actually, such beautiful women. Most of the men are trolls."

"I've always wondered what it would be like to be beautiful,"

Becky said, emerging from the stall. The bathroom was fragrant with enormous arrangements of fresh lilies, and she dried her hands on a linen towel.

"It wouldn't be so wonderful, I don't think. Most of the beautiful women I know end up marrying distinctly unattractive men, just because they're rich. They're all quite miserable."

"You're beautiful," Becky said.

"Really? I never think of myself that way. Thank you," Annabelle said, inspecting herself in the mirror. She bestowed a smile of such sincerity on Becky that it made her feel sorry for kissing Warner. "Let's take a walk through the restaurant, shall we, before we go back to the table? I'm curious to see if there's anyone we know."

Becky followed the older woman as she sashayed through the restaurant, which was larger than she'd first thought, with private tables tucked into corners under overhangings of flowers and vines. Table after table of candlelit faces peered up at Annabelle.

When they were almost at the terrace entrance Annabelle bent over for a second look at a man in a pink Polo shirt who was sitting with two women in silence. "Jason, is that you?"

"Annabelle!" The man rose, flustered, and they kissed each other's cheeks in a polite display of affection. The women at the table, both short and pretty in a nondescript way, sipped from their drinks and stared down at their untouched plates. Becky stood in the background while Annabelle chatted with the man, and then followed her back to their table.

"Anyone here tonight?" Warner inquired of his wife, handing a cellphone back to the waiter.

"No one you know. Although I did see one person I know," she admitted, sipping from her wineglass. "A former lover, Warner, from a long time ago. He was having a rather uncomfortable meal with his current girlfriend *and* his ex-girlfriend! That was one table where no one was having any fun."

"Excuse me." Warner left the table, cigarette in hand.

"Where's he going?" Becky asked.

"Oh, off to have a look at Jason, I suspect." Annabelle beckoned to the waiter for more wine.

Becky's head was swimming, her vision felt as though it were coming and going in the candlelit darkness. Annabelle's face slipped back and forth in front of her, a pale, lurid mask. The odour of the flowers was overwhelming.

Warner returned to the table, his curiousity apparently satisfied. Annabelle smiled at Warner, indulging his jealousy, then turned to Becky. "Tell me, how did you meet Howard and Georgia?"

"How do people meet? I don't know, around. At a reception, I guess. Howard's someone in the community, and I've written about him in my column. Then I got to know him and Georgia, and we go for dinner sometimes. They've had me over to their house. They're very generous people."

"Yes, I've been friends with Georgia for years. She's been so good for Howard," Annabelle said. "I wouldn't have thought I'd be saying this years ago, when I had a crush on him, but I'm happy he's found someone like her."

"I don't wish to interrupt, but—Rebecca, when I was walking through the restaurant I ran into someone I thought you should interview for your column. Will you join me for a minute and I'll introduce you?" Warner said, half-rising from his chair.

Once they were away from the table Warner wrapped his arm around her. She was dizzy and laughing, and they swayed among the tables, heedless of who might be watching when he bent to kiss her. She could not get enough of Warner, his warmth, his hands, his lips, his wonderful face. Brian no longer existed for her.

She wanted it to last forever. She wanted him to say something to her, to tell her what he felt for her, to make her feel loved. But after a while he steered them back towards the table, where his wife sat with her head bent.

"Are you okay?" Becky asked breathlessly, flopping down into her chair, her body tingling from Warner's touch. "You look tired."

"Oh, *yes*." She raised her face. Her lips were twisted. "Tired. Yes, I am tired. I'm tired of not having my clothes in one place. I'm tired of travelling back and forth, looking for a house here, trying to get moved into this town. I'm sorry, Becky, I'm just not up for dinner after all."

"Let's go then, darling," Warner suggested. Becky, watching him closely for any sign of their encounter moments ago, saw that he was smooth, unperturbed.

It was mid-August before she saw Warner and Annabelle again. In the meantime, Brian was staying in an adobe house in New Mexico which he rented for several months each year to work on his paintings. He sent a plane ticket for Becky to visit him for a holiday, and she was curious about what it would be like to spend two weeks of uninterrupted time with him. Everything could happen between them in the desert, or they could look at each other and realize there was nothing there.

Before leaving for New Mexico, she went to the opening of a musical at a new theatre in town. It was an extravagant, black-tie event, and she invited a friend of hers along. Dylan was a doctor she had met while researching an article on AIDS; he headed a research clinic on sexually transmitted diseases, and the two of them had become friends during the course of their interview and a spontaneous lunch afterwards. He was bright, lustful and, as he liked to say, "Deep down, I'm superficial." She had seen him work his way through a string of beautiful girlfriends—ex-models, hostesses in upscale restaurants, actresses—dropping them at the first hint of marriage. "Why make one person miserable when I could make so many happy?" But he had a heart of gold where his friends were concerned, and she was grateful that their relationship had remained on that level.

It was on the second-floor lobby that she saw Warner. Dylan was buying their drinks, and she waited for him against the balcony that overlooked the twin marble staircases that diverged upwards from the entrance. On the opposite wall, a brilliant segmented mirror, reflecting light from the skylight above, also reflected the crush of guests—each several times over, in an odd optical illusion. Becky could see herself in two different panels of the towering mirror. When the soft bell rung for the guests to take their seats, she and Dylan turned to the orchestra-level doors, and ran straight into Warner and Annabelle.

"Hello, Becky." Annabelle smiled and then strode past them with her chin lifted and her eyes focused ahead.

"Darling! So good to see you!" Warner embraced her warmly. His bright eyes searched her face, and he seemed overjoyed to see her. "And who is this sophisticated young man you're with?"

Becky introduced them, and then they were swept along with the crowd. She and Dylan took their seats in centre row.

Warner and Annabelle were in the aisle, trying to disengage themselves from a conversation with another couple, examining their tickets to find their row and seat numbers. As it turned out, they were seated at the end of Becky's row.

Annabelle sat stiffly, staring straight ahead, her back erect. She wore a trim black suit, and held the pelt of a brown mink in her lap. Warner leaned forward and smiled at Becky across his wife.

"Interesting," Dylan commented, observing. "There seems to be some chemistry between you and Warner. Am I right?"

"Well . . ." But then the lights went down. During the two-hour performance Becky remained aware of Warner and Annabelle, close to her; she could see them in her peripheral vision. Annabelle had put on glasses when the musical started, and the frames winked in the dim light. Warner was wearing an exquisitely tailored black suit; the triangle of silk in his breast pocket glowed, it was so white. His face grew bright and dim with the flickering of the stage lights. Becky watched him, and she wondered then if she was in love. If love was the pounding of her heart, the dampness of her palms, her breathlessness? In that sea of men and women in all their finery inside the theatre, there was but one person for her: Warner Maclean.

She stayed in her seat at intermission. Annabelle drifted down to the front row and then off to the far aisle; everywhere she went she was greeted, kissed, embraced. Taller than the women around her, she bore herself like a homecoming queen, inclining her head, bestowing her smile here and there like a benediction. Becky recalled what Warner had said of his wife during one of their conversations: "Whenever we go out socially, she's mobbed. I guess that's what I get for marrying a beautiful woman." His voice had had a curiously flat quality to it. Now she looked across at him, sitting in the aisle seat alone; he seemed to be looking back at her, and it was a moment before she realized he was actually looking beyond her, to where his wife was standing, surrounded.

The summer ended and two weeks with Brian in New Mexico became the beginning of a serious relationship, one that involved travelling with him to his exhibitions. Everything was changing, and she thought of Warner only intermittently, concluding that he was never right for her regardless of what she felt when she was with him. He already had a wife, and his life was one she did not understand. With Brian, there was something real. She didn't know if it was love—it wasn't what she had felt for Warner in the theatre, not that pulse-pounding breathlessness—but something deep and calm and reliable. To accommodate her travels with Brian, she changed her weekly column to a monthly appearance and focused her attentions instead on freelance articles.

Warner called whenever she was in town. Although he and Annabelle had bought a house, he always rang from work or his cellular phone.

"Things at my company aren't going as well as I'd hoped," was all he'd say when she inquired. "But how are you, my darling? What is happening in your exciting life?"

They were rarely in town at the same time; when she saw him next it was during intermission on the opening night of a play at the theatre. She was standing in the lobby with a talk-show host whom she had dated a few times before meeting Brian. Warner's face was a beacon in the crowd, and the moment she saw him she realized how much she had missed him.

"Darling. It's you." He held her hands and kissed her cheeks, keeping her at a distance.

"How are you? Where's Annabelle?"

"She's in the washroom. What's happening? Tell me, what exotic places have you been to with Mr. Thompson since we last spoke?" His face was tanned; he and Annabelle had just returned from a vacation in the Mediterranean; he looked well. It wasn't until he had excused himself to look for Annabelle that the talk-show host, even now unable to contain the jealousy that had been so off-putting when he and Becky were dating, began to pry.

"Who was that man who kissed you? He looked like a rich banker."

"His name's Warner Maclean."

"Oh yes, I've heard of him. I hear the company's in mighty big trouble," he concluded with a smirk. Becky looked at him in surprise, but she had no opportunity to ask any questions because the second act was about to begin.

"It's a beautiful September afternoon, we're both in town for a change, and I think we must have a drink and talk," Warner declared. "This is not a day for staying indoors, this is a day for being alive!"

It was windy by the water, and Becky had to keep her hands in the pockets of her skirt to prevent it from blowing up around her waist as they walked to their table on the deck, Warner's shoes tapping on the wooden floor. They ate appetizers and drank white wine, alternately removing and donning sunglasses as clouds blew over and past the sun. All around them was the murmuring ocean, the mountains, the waterfront homes ringing the shore.

They talked of their travels, and when she asked about his company he said that he had quit. "It was a mess. The entire venture was a mistake. Actually, some people pushed me out, accused me of all sorts of horrible things. But we won't dwell on that, not on this beautiful day."

"What do you plan to do next?"

"I'm thinking about that at the moment, examining my options. Nothing appeals to me just yet. I'm spending more time at home, reading, considering. Darling, bring your wine and let's walk out onto the pier."

They walked past the boats, out to where the waves crashed and slid beneath their feet. She kept pace with his footsteps, slow, measured; she listened to the sound of his breathing and tried to breathe with him. A feeling of tranquillity bloomed in her chest. She wanted the pier to stretch out into the middle of the ocean, to go on forever—his steps next to hers, his sleeve brushing hers as they walked.

"You must remember this moment, always," he said, next to her. His voice was quiet, intense. "Promise me."

Becky nodded. "I will."

They began walking back along the pier. He lit a cigarette and drew on it in silence for a while. "I am a little impatient with myself these days," he said eventually. "I am blessed with a wonderful Harvard education, a house that is a mansion, good friends and connections—yet I don't seem to know what I want to do next in my life."

"It hasn't been that long since you left your company. You can afford to do nothing. You can retire."

"Dear God, spare me. Yes, I suppose you're right, it hasn't been that long." He continued smoking, deep in thought, until they reached the parking lot. Then he took her arm and pointed across an expanse of grass to a bench overlooking the beach and the water.

"Let's not leave yet. We'll sit there, and you'll tell me more about your relationship with Mr. Thompson. I have some of his work in my house. Congratulations on your good fortune, Rebecca. Are you in love?"

Becky thought about that while they walked across the grass. "I don't know," she said at last. "It's a love of sorts. He's a kind person, we travel well together, and he's been good for me. I certainly tell him I love him. It's not love the way I've felt it before," she said, and then she looked at Warner. He could have said something at that moment and she would have responded.

He took off his hat and set it on his lap. He stared out at the water and said nothing.

"What about you and Annabelle? Are you happy?"

"It changes, day to day," he said. "She can be very difficult. Of course, Reginald's death is something that changed her." He paused. "Have you ever thought of suicide, Rebecca?"

She glanced at him in surprise, but his profile gave nothing away. "Well, when I was a teenager, I guess. Doesn't everyone, when they're teenagers?"

"I've had times in my life when I considered it as an option," he said, still not looking at her. "When I was close. But I've always managed to pull back from that edge."

He changed the subject then, and a while later they walked back across the parking lot. "Tap, tap, tap," he smiled, echoing his shoes. He drove her home, and when she asked him in for a drink, he declined.

"No, Annabelle went out for dinner this evening, but she'll be home by now. I should be with her. Let me walk you to your door, darling."

At the front gate they embraced, and she did not want to let him go. "I've missed you," she ventured. She wished she could say more.

The leaves had already turned when Warner called again. He was as charming as ever, interested in Becky's work and friendships and her relationship with Brian, but he sounded less upbeat when she asked after him. It seemed Warner and Annabelle were spending more time apart—he went back to Cardinal for a few weeks without her, she travelled to the Blair estate further east without him. "But we're not separating or anything like that. I'm madly in love with my wife," he assured her.

He avoided her questions about his work, saying only that he was having difficulties which involved many lawyers and would take a while for him to sort out. "It's taking its toll on me. I've already lost ten pounds. But, I needed to."

Becky didn't insist on prying; she was eager to talk to him about her own problems. Brian was mentioning marriage all the time now, and she vacillated between agreeing to consider his proposal and changing the subject. It was with Warner, rather than her girlfriends, whom she chose to share her ambivalences; he listened to her intently, as though it were his future they were discussing.

"I don't know, darling," he said at last. "I don't think you should marry him. Everything I've heard you say about him, I think it would be a mistake. It's the way you talk about him, I don't hear any passion, any fire. You should feel like this person is your soulmate, you should be wholeheartedly in love with him, head over heels in love."

"Maybe it's normal to have doubts."

"I never had any doubts, with my wives."

The question of marriage, and the nature of the love she felt for Brian, loomed over her until she found it impossible to concentrate on anything else. Was he the person with whom she wanted to share her life? She did want to get married; she felt safe, comfortable with him. He would not hurt or abandon her. She thought of Warner leaving his girlfriend after meeting Annabelle at a reception, leaving his girlfriend that very night.

One afternoon, she went to visit a massage therapist after working long hours on her computer. As the woman kneaded the knots in her shoulders, a building, unstoppable clamour of anxiety rose in her, making her palms sweat and her stomach cramp. It escalated until she felt blind with it and had to ask the woman to stop. The therapist, who had crystals dangling at her windowpanes and a tape playing rainforest sounds on the stereo, propped her up in a chair and insisted on trying a calming technique on her. She instructed Becky to visualize her worries and then expel them to a far corner of the room.

"What is causing the panic? Can you see it and throw it up to that corner?"

Becky rolled her eyes, but she cooperated. She sat up straight and breathed deeply several times. She focused on the corner of the room and saw her fear—marrying Brian, and possibly making the greatest mistake of her life.

"Now think of something wonderful. Something that makes you feel perfectly safe, warm, happy," the therapist soothed.

Becky closed her eyes. She searched for a while through her memories and experiences, but none seemed powerful enough to counter her fear. An image at last floated up, and then what she wanted became clear.

It had been Warner Maclean, all along.

She next heard from him late one night, while he was driving alone around the city.

"I'm not happy at all right now," he confessed. "I'll be going back to Cardinal for a while, I don't know how long. I need to sit among my things, and be alone. Maybe I won't return, I don't know."

"What about Annabelle?" Becky had never heard him so pessimistic. "Are you separating?"

"Well, I guess it's a separation if I'm there and she's here, isn't it? If you mean a formal one, no."

"Do you still love her?" Becky found herself holding her breath.

"Love." He paused; static filled the receiver. "I've finally come to a point in my life where I don't know what love is."

Becky felt her heart drop in disappointment. It had always seemed to her that Warner was certain of his emotions, when other men she knew weren't.

"Have you talked to her about all this?"

"Oh, of course. We've been talking and talking. Ad nauseam. At some point, words are useless. There are no more words to say."

Becky wanted to protest, but Warner said suddenly, "Where the hell am I? Oh, all right, this is the Safeway parking lot. I don't want the Safeway parking lot, how do I get out? Yes, darling, things are going very badly indeed. I am being accused of all sorts of unspeakable things. What is the world coming to? Now I am turning into a movie theatre, and what's playing? My God, something to do with the Holocaust. No, I don't have the stomach for that tonight."

She wanted to give something to him, words of comfort. She knew he kept a journal, a wine-coloured leatherbound book he had once pulled out to show her. "Have you been writing at all in your diary?"

"You mean, for *therapy*? For *catharsis*?" He laughed bitterly, a harsh sound that was new to her. "No. Words don't do any good, that's what I've discovered. Words are meaningless. I am going to go back to Cardinal and try to sort things out. I'll be back for short visits. I've still got a lot of business to tie up here even if I don't come back to stay."

"We should get together for a drink when you're back," she ventured.

"Darling, I couldn't imagine anything nicer." And then he was gone, to drive around aimlessly, she imagined, for a few more hours, or the rest of the night. The thought unsettled her—Warner Maclean, as susceptible to sorrow in work and love, as alone and lost, as anyone.

"Well, I was wondering what had happened to you," Rachel said to her at the gym. She paused by the chest-press machine where Becky was exercising. "I haven't seen you around much lately."

"Brian and I have been travelling a lot. And, I'm just lazy."

"You're not the only one. So, it sounds like things are pretty serious between you and Brian Thompson. I was driving downtown last week and I saw the two of you walking down the street, holding hands. It was just so sweet. Do I hear wedding bells?"

Becky laughed, brushing damp strands of hair off her forehead. "We're just having a good time right now, that's all. What's new with you? How's work? What kinds of stories are you covering?"

"The usual boring crap, nothing of interest to you. Unless— you know Warner Maclean, don't you? Right, you met him at the library opening. Well, he's in very big trouble. He was ousted from his company a few months ago," she said, her voice dropping to an excited whisper. "It seems one of the board members did a little background investigation on him, and discovered that he was under investigation for embezzling two million dollars from a capital corporation back East. The shit hit the fan, as you can imagine. Minority shareholders seized control and Warner was forced out. I wasn't the only one covering the story, it's been in all the business magazines. The court's already looking at freezing his assets, and if they find him responsible for what happened back East, it'll be game over. They'll start selling off everything he owns. The way it stands now, his name is already mud in this town. Poor Annabelle, I hear she's just having a fit."

At home in her apartment that night, Becky wrote Warner a note, which she faxed to Cardinal. "A business reporter I know told me about the troubles you've been having," she wrote. "I hope you're all right. Remember that no matter what happens we have only ourselves. It meant something to me, when you told me that. I hope it still means something to you."

It was the middle of the night where he was, but her fax machine rang minutes later. "My dear Rebecca," he wrote, "I haven't forgotten. I won't ever forget."

She did not know how to reach him, beyond that.

He called often, to inquire about her life. He asked so many questions that she was barely able to ask him any in return, and realized that was probably how he wanted it.

"I am not well, darling," he conceded when she pressed. "Physically, emotionally, spiritually, mentally—I am not well. Fighting this legal battle is taking everything out of me, and I'm not looking after myself properly. They are saying the worst things about me in the press. My God, I have had more bad publicity in the past few months than I thought possible. But enough of that, how are you? Tell me everything."

It was November when Becky attended a film festival party with Howard and Georgia. A band was playing in the hotel ballroom where the party was held—loud, swinging music that made it pointless to carry on a conversation. Becky wandered away from them and walked alone around the dark, cavernous room. Purple and lime strobe lights flashed like a headache. The tables were strewn with buckets of spilled popcorn, streamers, handfuls of glittering, cut-out stars. Men and women pushed past her, carrying glasses of champagne and plates piled with freshly carved roast beef and salads from the banquet table. Becky felt, inexplicably, sad. Brian was at home, sketching or, more likely, already asleep; he hated social events, hated the forced conversations, the fancy clothes, the pretensions. He would not have understood her attraction to someone like Warner, would never have considered Annabelle beautiful. "She doesn't look like she eats enough to keep body and soul together. You're much more beautiful than she is," he'd say.

It took her a moment to recognize Warner at the centre of the room. It couldn't be anyone else, with his fastidious suit and his cigarette, but he looked greatly diminished, and older. Perhaps it was the strobe lights, but his face was ashen, glossed over with perspiration.

"Warner, how are you?" She went to embrace him, and there was a moment of awkwardness as he took her hands instead, kissing her firmly on the cheek. Then she saw Annabelle behind him, the centre of attention in a backless floor-length sequinned gown that spilled down her body. Annabelle glanced at her, turned and drifted away.

"My dear, I am melancholy. But I am surviving."

"You've lost a lot of weight."

"Forty pounds. But now I have a hell of a physique! You should see me out of these clothes, I have the body of a young stud." He winked and pretended to strike a pose, and for a moment she relaxed, laughing. But when she looked at him again she was worried. He was carrying an ebony-handled cane, which he lent upon like an old man, smaller, deflated.

"Let me introduce you to my daughter," he said, resting one hand heavily on the shoulder of a slender adolescent. "Thirteen years old and already wearing two-inch heels, tsk!"

The girl had clear, olive-coloured skin; her legs were bare, and she wore a dress with a sailor collar and tiny polka dots. She wriggled shyly under his touch, glancing at Becky from under thick lashes. Looking at the two of them together, Becky was reminded of a picture she had lingered over in a Bible book that an aunt had given her when she was a child. The picture spread across two pages, portraying the arc of life—on the far left-hand side, a rosy infant on a knoll of grass. To his right was a child wearing short pants, then a straight-limbed student with earnest eyes, then a young man in a soldier's uniform, a new husband carrying a briefcase, and so on—the infant aging until, at the far right-hand corner, a gnarled old man stooped over a cane, and finally a crumbling skeleton on another knoll of grass. If the girl was the straight-limbed student, she thought, then who was Warner? Was he already the old man with the cane, the arc of his life nearly over?

"Where is Mr. Thompson tonight, darling? Is he here?"

"No, he hates going out if he doesn't have to. He's probably at home, sleeping. His idea of a perfect night is to have dinner at six and be in bed by eleven," she said, feeling disloyal.

"Hmm, that can't be too amusing for you. Are you still considering marriage?"

"Oh, we always have that conversation. Some days I think so. I've told you that I feel safe with him, and I care about him. Maybe that's good enough."

"Don't do it, darling." He exhaled cigarette smoke; she winced as it drifted in front of her, and he waved his hand under her nose. "Excuse me, I'm always doing this to you. Filthy habit. But listen to me, don't. It would be an absolute disaster. You're not in love with him, I don't hear that in your voice. If you get married, it would erode the friendship and caring that you do have. It would eat away at that, and you'd end up with nothing."

"But—"

"Darling, you don't seem happy." He considered her, and then he smiled. "You see, you never seem happy to me. Why is that?"

"That's not true. I am happy." She smiled defiantly, but he continued to observe her closely, as he always had. "You're the one I'm worried about."

"Yes, my affairs are not going as well as they could. I'm not well, either. I'm going back to Cardinal again, the day after tomorrow. Now you must excuse me," he said. He took her hands, pressed them, and she felt his familiar heat radiating through her. Then he wrapped his arms around her and held her close. "I must go look for Annabelle, perhaps she's talking to Howard. You look beautiful tonight, darling, you do," he murmured against her hair, and then he let her go.

In a few weeks, it would be Christmas. Brian was in New Mexico for the winter; she had flown down with him, spent two weeks in the desert, then explained that she wanted to return home to spend the holidays with her friends. There were parties and dinners she did not want to miss, social occasions which he would not enjoy. She promised to visit him again after the first of the year, and they planned a vacation for later that month. In the meantime he called her twice a day, and she thought sometimes that this was the best their relationship would ever get—missing each other, caring for each other at enough of a distance that they could live their own lives.

She thought, for a while, that Warner was doing better. He was considering purchasing a literary publishing house that had gone bankrupt. "Publishers, people in the arts—they're soft," he chuckled over the phone. "They like to think of themselves as business people, but they're all soft when you compare them to the real world."

One afternoon he called her on his way to the airport; he was flying to Hong Kong, where there was a possibility that he would head the first non-state-governed cable television network in China. "If this works out, I could stand to make a fortune," he enthused. "I mean, a fortune. Billions! I've also taken up a visiting professorship at a business school back East—they're paying me a ridiculous amount for the little work I have to do." Becky was glad for him, and not surprised; she could imagine him as a tycoon in a glass tower in Hong Kong, speaking the Chinese he had learned as a student at Harvard.

But when he returned to Cardinal, he was downcast. "It didn't work out. It's not the right position for me. Those people don't know what they're doing." A tiny doubt entered Becky's mind—had he rejected their offers, as he claimed, or had they rejected him? He called her several times a week, and their conversations began to disturb her. They were less like talks than interrogations. He asked her one question after another, barely giving her time to reply. Had she seen Howard recently? Did Howard mention him ever? What about the woman she knew from the gym—the business reporter—what did she say about Warner? Did she have other friends in the business community who knew about him? What did they say about him behind his back?

"I can't come to see you, darling," he said when she asked when he would be returning. "People hate me now in your town. I'm vilified. My God, if they saw me walking down the street, all hell would break loose. No, I simply can't go back."

"What about your family?"

"My family is all over the place, my dear. Annabelle? She has her own problems right now. You see, she's convinced I've brought all this misfortune down upon her, that I've given her a bad name because things that happened a long, long time ago are being dredged up now, and she's guilty by association because she's married to me. I don't know what happened to our vows. I thought that when you married someone you were with them for richer or for poorer, for better or for worse. I was there for her, and I put up with her family."

"What are you going to do?"

"Darling, I have no idea." He paused, and for a while there was only the faint hum of the long-distance line. "Rebecca, do you ever think about suicide? Now, I mean."

She took a breath. She felt as if she were walking on ground that might give underneath her if she took a wrong step. "No, not now. But I was a pretty miserable teenager, and once or twice I came close."

"My God, really?"

"I would probably just have taken a bottle of aspirin, though, expecting to wake up in the hospital. You know, a cry for attention."

"Mm. Why didn't you go through with it? What stopped you?"

She sighed, hoping he was not seeking her counsel. "Maybe I was afraid of succeeding."

"I've been thinking about suicide," he said finally. "The way I see it, I have three options: I can declare bankruptcy and start over again; I can fight this court injunction and spend all my remaining money and energy doing it; or I can kill myself. I'm sixty years old, darling. It might take more than I have to start over again. It's fine when you're a young man of forty, let's say. I've done it before, I've lost my money and gotten it back. Now, I don't know."

Becky was not as disturbed by his disclosure as others might have been and this, she realized, was perhaps why he told her. She was not about to raise an alarm, call the hospital, the men in white coats. She did not know any of his friends, his family or his social circle—she was outside of his world, not connected to the people he had to impress. She was certainly not going to talk to Annabelle. And, she believed that people who talked about suicide never attempted it. She recalled how he had insisted on showing her the building he was thinking of buying before taking her to dinner that night after work. The talk of suicide had the same element of self-display to it.

The next time he called it was cold on both coasts, and he was looking out at acres of snow from his home office. "For the first time in my life, I'm humiliated," he said. "Annabelle's friends are saying that I've ruined her life. They insist that she should divorce me. She says she's only ever really been married once, and that was to Reginald. I'm just devastated."

"Are you still in love with her?"

"Love? Love. I'm in love with my wife, I'm in love with you. It's ridiculous. Now, when I need her most, she isn't here for me. I suppose I can't blame her, she refuses to see what I'm going through. I'm not going to last much longer, Rebecca. I'm almost ready to end it all, darling, leave the party before the gin runs out."

Becky had stopped listening. All she heard was, "I'm in love with you." She looked at the receiver in her hand. It was no longer the right time, it had come too late. Warner's desperation silenced her; she was so afraid of saying the wrong thing that she said nothing.

"What are you doing for Christmas?" he asked. He listened as she told him about the dinners and parties to which she had been invited. Then she heard him exhale. "Come out here for Christmas. Please come, darling. Get on a plane tonight and I'll pick you up at the airport. We'll stay a few days here at the house, then we'll drive down to my vacation property in the South. We'll sit in the sun, drink rum and talk. We'll spend the rest of my money and go out with a bang. You can return in the new year, if you want, but you might decide you never want to leave. How does that sound?"

It was the invitation she had been waiting for, but now she hesitated. She had a brief image of her and Warner, together, in the Charleston house where, she knew, he and Annabelle had been married. She thought of how they would talk late into the night, how she would lay her head on his shoulder, how he would hold her close and she would breathe in his scent of wool and tobacco. She closed her eyes and shook her head.

"I'm not sure I can. I've promised all my friends I'll be at their dinner parties. It would be rude to cancel at the last minute. I've got several articles I'm supposed to write. And then there's Brian."

"Ah yes, Mr. Thompson. On top of everything else, now people will accuse me of breaking up your relationship with Brian Thompson. Darling, you make up your mind. Do what's right for you, all right? I don't want to pressure you to do anything. But I very much need to see you. You can write your articles here. I promise you'd get them written twice as fast in my office. Call me later on and tell me what you've decided. I'll be here."

Becky wanted to go. But she knew that once she was with Warner, alone, he would be in control and, because she was weaker than he was, she would succumb to his wishes. If he kissed her, if he touched her, she would follow him to his bed. If he asked her to marry him, she would say yes. She would never be able to explain his hold over her to anyone, least of all to Brian, who had given her no reason to betray him.

Howard called that afternoon, to ask if she would join his family for Christmas Day dinner.

"You're not going down to New Mexico, are you?"

"No, I was planning to be here. I'd like to come." Becky hesitated, then added, "It's just—Howard, you know Warner Maclean."

"Warner Maclean." His voice was full of dismay. "What's Warner done now."

"Well, he's asked me to spend Christmas with him at Cardinal. He wants to drive down South together, and—"

"Is he still with Annabelle?"

"Not at the moment. They've separated for a while. It sounds like it's over between them."

"I don't trust Warner," he said, with a bluntness she had not heard before from him. "He's slippery. He's gotten himself into a lot of trouble, and it's his own damn fault. Georgia and I saw Annabelle socially last week, and she was despondent. He keeps telling people that she's psychologically unwell, which makes her worse. We think he's taken a chunk out of her financially, too. Those two should never have gotten married. Becky, didn't I introduce you to Warner?"

"You did."

"It was at the library opening, of course. I should watch who I introduce you to in the future."

"I like Warner," she tried to explain. "We talk. He's not very happy right now."

"And so he shouldn't be, he's created a hell of a mess." His voice took on an edge of anger, which passed. "Becky, I am not living your life. Far be it for me to tell you what to do. But I'd steer clear of Warner Maclean. I don't like him. From where I sit, going to Cardinal to see Warner would not be my idea of a sane thing to do."

It was late at night when she called him from her bed. She took a breath, and said, "Warner, I can't. There's research I have to do here for the articles, people I have to interview. I'd feel terrible jamming out on my friends at the last minute. But look, if you're not doing anything for Christmas, you can come here. I'm sure you'd be welcome to come with me to some of these dinner parties. You can sleep on my couch." She laughed unconvincingly.

"No. You don't want to come," he said flatly. "If you did, you'd find a way. I'll make other plans."

"Warner—"

"Rebecca, you've decided what's best for you." He sounded sad. "I'm not going to ask you to do anything you don't want to do. It's your decision, sweet thing."

When he hung up, she thought of a poem by Stephen Dobyns that she had read years ago. "The City of Missed Opportunities" was set in a place after death, a purgatory whose inhabitants said and did all the things they regretted not having said or done in their lives. She remembered a man in the poem who tattooed his forehead with the words, "Madge, don't shoot."

"Madge, don't shoot," she whispered into the silent phone.

In January, first Becky, then Brian, came down with the flu, and they had to postpone her trip to New Mexico; she stayed at home, working, pleased to have some time to herself. When

Warner called it was to resume what felt to her like an interrogation.

"How was your dinner with Howard and Georgia, en famille?"

"Very nice. It was lovely."

"Hmm. And what did you talk about?"

"Oh, everything. Books, travel, music, politics, people—"

"People, hmm? Did you mention me at all?"

In fact they had spent some time discussing Warner—the damage he had done to Annabelle, how he could not be trusted. "He's a slippery one," Georgia had said. "Oh yes, I agree with you, Becky, he's charming and he's absolutely brilliant, but he's dangerous. I sensed something wrong when I saw one of the letters he addressed to Howard. How did it go, love? 'My dear Howard.' It just didn't sound—right. He's too slick, we don't trust him."

"You were mentioned just in passing." She hated it, that she was lying to him. "Howard asked how you were doing, if you were still with Annabelle. I said I didn't think so, that the last I heard you were at Cardinal and you weren't feeling that well."

"Not feeling well, hmm?" He paused. "Yes, I suppose you could say I'm not feeling well."

He said he had spent an uneventful holiday, visiting friends. He was planning to return after all, within the next few weeks, and he wanted to make sure Becky would be in town when he did. "I must see you then. Do take care of yourself in the meantime.

Take very, very good care of yourself, darling. I wish you all the best in your life, with your work, with love, with everything. I want nothing but the best for you, Rebecca."

This was how he had come to end his conversation with her. As though they would never see each other again, it occurred to her, but she refused to think about it.

It was a beautiful winter morning when he came to her door. The wind swept everything clean so that the edges of the buildings serrated the tile-blue sky. The air was crisp, sweet in her throat like the first bite of a harvest apple.

He was driving an old ivory Bentley, with big, boxy windows like television screens. Rectangular mirrors adorned the sides of the back seat, where a dog with floppy chenille ears barked piercingly as she got into the car.

"Shut up, Gatsby! Shut up! Stupid dog. How are you, my dear," he said, reaching over to rest his hand against Becky's cheek. "You look wonderful, darling."

Warner had lost more weight. He looked shrunken in his camel-hair coat, his face sallow and thin.

"We will do several things today. First, I want to go look at a warehouse building I'm considering buying to renovate as retail space. Then, you'll bear with me while I run some errands, and after that we'll get a bite to eat."

They parked in front of a warehouse where some Chinese

errand boys came out to ogle the car. The owner's son had a key to the upstairs floor and led Warner and Becky into the old-fashioned elevator that clanked slowly up to the lofts, which were crammed with boxes of merchandise. Becky wandered through the rooms behind Warner, watching him. His walk had become the shuffle of an old man wearing bedroom slippers; Becky actually glanced down at his feet, to see that he wasn't. All his motions were dazed, lethargic, as though he were wading through water; when he went to withdraw a business card to give to the building owner, he patted all his pockets dreamily, extracting money clips and scraps of paper and cigarettes, and it took him another few minutes to locate his pen.

"Well, that wasn't bad at all, that place," he concluded as they got into the car. The dog started a frenzy of barking again, trying valiantly to leap into the front seat, and he pushed it back with the palm of his hand. "Gatsby, shut up! Now really, I mean it. Silly dog doesn't know friends from enemies. Hmm, I like that building. It just might work out. Of course, my assets are frozen worldwide, so that means I have no capital to put up. It's harder to buy things without capital, but it can be done."

Becky still believed he could do anything he wanted. "I'm afraid I'll never know anything about business."

"It's simple. Buy, sell, buy, sell. That's all there is to it."

They sailed through the downtown streets in the Bentley. It was like sitting in a plush igloo; its creamy movement soothed her, made her feel cocooned. While they drove, passersby and other drivers turned to peer inside the car windows at them, and she wondered if they were being envied.

They stopped at an antique store where Warner fondled canes, ivory cigarette holders, leather cigar cases. "I love to shop!" he exclaimed. He turned to grin impishly at Becky, and for a moment he was entirely his former self, delighted with everything, on top of the world. "I am like a child in shops. Isn't this wonderful? Are you having fun?" She watched him indulgently, as if he were indeed a child, pleased by his pleasure. When he carried his purchases to the counter he extracted several gold cards from his wallet, and she looked away as they were all, one after the other, rejected.

He seemed unembarrassed, and ended up relinquishing most of the merchandise, paying only for a plastic cigarette holder and a pouch of tobacco with money in his wallet. They walked back out into the sunshine, and he bit down on the cigarette holder. "Darling, I was robbed over Christmas. I had seven thousand dollars in cash in my briefcase, clothes, a twelve-hundred-dollar Hermès scarf I'd just bought for Annabelle, presents for the children—all gone. They broke into my car while I was parked in front of a restaurant and took everything."

She did not know whether or not to believe him, and she didn't know what upset her more—that he might be lying to her, or that he was telling the truth and she doubted him.

"I am not well, darling. I keep losing things—cigarette

holders, pens, lighters. I seem to keep leaving things behind someplace and then having to buy replacements. I don't know what's happening to me."

"How are things with Annabelle?"

"Terrible, at the moment. We had another screaming fight last night, nothing has been resolved. Let's go and get the car washed, shall we, darling? Then we'll find a place for lunch. I must talk to you. Personally, I mean." He reached over and touched her sleeve.

They drove through the poorest part of the city to look for a car wash. The Bentley was as conspicuous as if it were a float in a parade, and Becky held her breath as he manoeuvred the car slowly through the skid-row streets.

At the rundown car wash the employees approached the car tentatively, as though it were a mirage that might vanish if they came too close. Warner rolled down the window, attempting to give instructions, but the dog panicked at the strange faces and began a frenzy of ear-splitting barks. He rolled the window up and down several times, attempting to communicate, and when the animal only got more hysterical he turned suddenly and shouted.

"Gatsby, Jesus Christ!" Becky had never heard him swear, and she watched, feeling sick, as he started smacking the animal viciously about its head while the car wash employees stood outside, giggling nervously. "Stupid dog! Stupid idiot dog, shut up now! You are driving me mad, Gatsby, I mean it, sit down and shut up!"

The dog whimpered, cowering from the blows, yet when Warner unrolled the window again it tensed and then let loose another volley of desperate barks, helpless in its desire to protect its master.

"Gatsby, I know you are just trying to look after me, but you really are a stupid dog," he said in a measured voice. The storm had passed. "Rebecca, excuse me, but this dog doesn't know when to stop. It thinks everyone is out to hurt me."

They remained in the car while he steered it through the wash, silencing Gatsby with one last, brutal smack that left the dog curled up on the back seat. Becky looked at Warner, who folded his hands on the wheel and stared through the windshield.

"I'm wildly in love with Annabelle," he said quietly. "I've made mistakes with my other wives, I always had girlfriends and that never did any good. If I had it to do over again, I wouldn't have had the affairs. But I've been faithful to Annabelle, absolutely."

The car passed into a torrent of water that crashed upon the hood like hail. She gazed through the windshield, sheeted with water. He was silent next to her, huddled in his coat, collapsed inward. She felt frightened and unbearably sad. She wanted to reach for him, take his hand or touch his cheek, but it would have been like touching someone who was naked while she herself was clothed.

They drove back downtown for lunch. It was early afternoon

and the first truly beautiful day in months of winter—sunlight glittered across the water, the sea and sky were variations of cobalt and marine. The interior of the car became so bright that she had to reach for her sunglasses.

"This city is tremendous, isn't it?" he mused. "I've been all around the world, and this is one of the most beautiful cities I have ever seen." He sighed. "It's odd, then, that the saddest events of my life should have happened here."

He took her to a diner on a busy street, where they slid into yellow plastic booths and ordered the all-day breakfast specials. The restaurant with the luxurious, candlelit terrace and the obsequious waiters seemed a world away. Warner buttered a triangle of toast and chewed mechanically. "Ah, this is my first food in three days."

"Warner," Becky said, concerned, "I can't be your mother." It was not what she had intended to say, yet somehow, once the words were out, she saw that it was. She wondered what her attachment to Warner really was, when now she felt herself shrinking back from him, detaching. Was it in an effort to protect herself, or did she care so little about him? She looked at him across the Formica tabletop and realized that along the way something had changed, so that now she was glad he was Annabelle's responsibility. He was Annabelle's husband, Becky had no husband.

They ate between snatches of conversation that, for the first time in their friendship, was stilted and forced. They had always been able to talk and now Becky wondered if he sensed her wariness. He watched her, with an air of resignation, she thought.

"The problem is, I wear people out," he said, gazing at her with a small, tired smile. "I've worn out everyone who has ever loved me."

Becky chewed and swallowed. The scrambled eggs felt leaden inside her stomach.

"People are wrong about me," Warner said suddenly. "I know that they think I'm calculating, that I'm slippery and scheming. But I'm not. I'm gullible. I take everyone at face value."

Becky could not meet his eyes. She was afraid that, somehow, she had betrayed him. "I have to admit, I've never thought of you as gullible."

"But I am." He looked beyond her, to a past she did not share. "That's what's wrong with me, I've always believed everything people told me. That's been my most serious mistake in life."

She excused herself to use the unisex washroom at the rear of the restaurant. She squeezed the door shut and stood in the bathroom that was no bigger than a closet, looking at herself in the mirror above the stained porcelain sink. She was glad she had not gone to Warner at Christmas, she saw now that he would have consumed her, worn her out. "Beware the vortex," Howard had said to her, and she understood now—the vortex was this spinning, this downward tug of another person's misery. It was the murderous clutch of the nearly drowned. But by not trying to save him she would be left with the guilt of the bystander who chose to look on and do nothing.

She returned reluctantly to the table where Warner was looking down at his empty plate, twisting his wedding ring around and around on his finger. When she asked to see it he pulled it off easily and placed it in her palm. It was a plain gold band, unremarkable; it could have been given or received by anyone. She held it back out to him, expecting him to take it from her, but instead he simply extended his ring finger. She was compelled to push it back down his finger, and there was something so embarrassingly intimate about this that she blushed and looked away. *I do.*

She struggled for something to say. "I'm off to New Mexico next week to see Brian. Things are still the same between us, and I still don't know what to do. He adores me, which is very seductive. He's sort of like an uncle to me."

"Darling, I used to think marriage meant something. That it was the most important thing in the world. So I wanted you to be careful. But I don't know what I think any more."

"Would it make a difference if things were going better between you and Annabelle?"

"It would make all the difference in the world. It would change everything." He put his hands on the table and pushed himself up from the booth. His face had darkened and he looked completely defeated. "We have to go. I must pick up my daughter from class. Marry your Mr. Thompson. If he loves you, if he can take care of you, then why not."

Becky was startled. She realized she had never wanted to hear this from Warner. "Do you really think I should?"

"It's not my decision, Rebecca," he said, seeming suddenly tired of her.

They walked out into the sunny downtown street. In front of the cafés, men and women were sitting around plastic tables, drinking low-fat lattes and fruit smoothies, wearing shades and tilting their faces up at the light. Joggers ran past, and sunlight bounced off the bumpers of the slow-moving traffic. If it had been warm, and green, the afternoon would have looked like summer. Warner put his arm around her shoulders as they walked back to the car. He squeezed her close, and a shadow of his former smile crossed his lips.

"You'll sort everything out," he said.

He stopped the car in the street outside her building, and they both got out. The cold winter sunlight shone on the Bentley, refracted from the windows of the thirty-storey towers on all sides of them. It stood between them, like a mirror or a pane of glass. Becky wanted to say something, felt a pressure inside her chest to speak, but she did not. Finally she asked, "What are you going to do?"

"I don't know." He shook his head. "I have no idea. Oh, maybe I'll fight it all, just for the hell of it."

"Where are you staying tonight?"

"I don't know. Two nights ago I was so suicidal that I drove to Emergency and asked to be admitted. But the psychiatrist told me I wasn't sick enough. So I was turned away."

The pressure building inside her closed her throat. She wanted to offer him something, but she had nothing to give him. There was a divide between them, and she saw now that it had nothing to do with money—it had to do with whatever separated the sick from the world of the living, with its minor preoccupations, to which she belonged.

He was smiling at her sadly. She refused to think that this might be the last time she would see him.

"Warner, if there's anything I can do to help." She paused, wondering what the limits were of what she would do for him. She realized that she no longer trusted him, that in this way she had become like everyone else in his life. "You'll let me know, won't you? It's just, I don't have any money or anything."

He started to laugh. "Darling, you couldn't make enough money in your entire life for what I need now." He held her against him, and she felt his warmth, his breath, and the faint, muffled beat of his pulse, far away. When they drew apart he took her hands between his and gazed into her eyes. His look was still steady, piercing, and it held hers with a tensile strength. The winter sun lit his face so brightly that she could not look at him.

"Look after yourself, Rebecca. I want nothing but good things to happen to you. Be happy, darling."

At the last moment, she wanted to reach out to him. There

was still time, she could still say something. But she had to protect herself against him, as surely as if he meant to harm her. She could not let him overpower her in his own desperate struggle for oxygen, for the light glimmering above the surface of water. Her heart hammered with the desire to do something, but she stood still, forcing herself to be silent. He climbed back inside the antique Bentley. The car was so beautiful that, she thought with a sudden leap of faith that absolved her, it would keep him safe. He would divorce Annabelle, return to Cardinal, start over. He would die when he was eighty-eight years old, enjoying a double shot of Bombay Sapphire, his beautiful young wife weeping by his bedside.

A week later, in the adobe house in New Mexico, Becky had a dream so vivid that it woke her in the middle of the night. Warner, thin, grey-faced, was being led away from her by several black-dressed men down a narrow alley. The light in the dream was bluish, twilight, and they seemed to be in a foreign city—there were cobblestones on the streets, and the buildings around them were old and shuttered. She felt that he was dying, and that there was something important she had to tell him.

"I've always loved you," she said and, in the dream, it was true. There was no doubt, no confusion.

He turned, and for a moment he looked straight at her. His

eyes softened, and he smiled. It was an absolution. "Yes, I know that. And I've always held it very close to my heart," he said simply. His words gave her peace, and she watched the men lead him away.

Pale grey light filled the high-ceilinged room when she woke. Brian lay next to her on his back, his mouth half-open, snoring. His black hair was tousled on his forehead, and his cheek wrinkled from the pillow. As though he felt her watching him, even in sleep, he turned over with a sigh and reached for her hand under the covers. "I love you, Becky," he whispered. She lay like that until dawn, holding his hand, listening to the tap of the eucalyptus against the windows and thinking of Warner.

It was Dylan who told her. He was the first to call when she returned home. Brian had taken her on a week's vacation to Bermuda, and the slow pace of that island had relaxed her so that for once she did not turn the key in her lock expecting a disaster, the way she usually did after she had been away—a flooded apartment, stolen equipment, messages from editors demanding rewrites to a dozen articles.

"Becky, I heard about Warner," he said.

She sat down, kicking off her shoes and tugging a blanket over her knees. It was winter here. "What's Warner done now?" She imagined an outrageous comeback—he'd been appointed president and CEO of a multinational corporation, he'd divorced Annabelle and married a twenty-year-old model, he'd made millions in one brilliant move on the stock market.

"You mean, you didn't hear?" Dylan's voice grew quiet. He was calling from his car phone, and the line was fuzzy.

She closed her eyes. The light between her eyelids was red and dark. She would not allow herself to feel anything.

"He killed himself. I can't believe someone didn't tell you. It happened a week ago, you'd just gone to Bermuda. He did it here, in the office he had at home, with a gun. It was in the papers, they interviewed his business associates and everyone was shocked, no one had a clue. His wife is devastated. Becky, I'm entering a tunnel right now, the cell isn't going to work. I'll call you back when I'm on the other side. Oh, I'm sorry you didn't know, I thought you knew."

"I didn't know," she managed to say. That was true, and yet it was also true that, of course, she had known all along, and done nothing.

ACKNOWLEDGEMENTS

I wish to thank Jim Sutherland at *Vancouver* magazine, for his invaluable support; the Varuna Writers Centre in Katoomba, Australia, for space to work; my literary agent, Denise Bukowski, for finding the right title; and Maya Mavjee and Martha Kanya-Forstner at Doubleday, for their diligent and perceptive editorial direction.